11/09

Caught in the Net of Deception

Rose Jackson-Beavers

&

Edward Booker

This book is a work of fiction. The incidents, characters and dialogue are products of the authors' imagination and are not to be interpreted as real. Any resemblance to actual people, living or dead is entirely coincidental.

Cover design by Majaluk.com

Manufactured in the United States of America

Library of Congress LCNN: 2009925348

ISBN 13:9780981648385

For information regarding discounts for bulk purchases, please contact Prioritybooks Publications. Visit our website at www.prioritybooks.com or info@prioritybooks.com

Caught in the Net of Deception

Published by
Prioritybooks Publications Missouri

Other books by Rose Jackson-Beavers

Sumthin' T' Say

Quilt Designs and Poetry Rhymes

A Hole in My Heart

Other books by Edward Booker

A Hole in My Heart

Acknowledgments

Rose and Edward would like to thank everyone who supported this book effort.

The Hood in Me
By Edward Booker

CHAPTER 1

Hit Me Up on MySpace

"Wut up, man? Wut it do?" Mike asked as Shawn approached him. Shawn was walking down the street smoking a strawberry swisher filled with a nic bag of weed.

"Let me hit that?" Mike asked.

"Alright," Shawn replied.

Mike took a strong puff. He really enjoyed the feeling of the smoke going smoothly down his throat. Smoking weed had become his passion lately. It made him feel better about his life and his problems. So who was he hurting by his enjoyment of weed?

Mike was hitting the cigarillo so hard that he forgot about Shawn, standing there waiting on him to pass it back.

"Don't hit it so hard, Mike," Shawn said as Mike began to cough.

"Man, that's some good stuff. Who you get that from?" Mike asked.

"From Taylor down the street. He got some fye this time, huh."

"Yep! So what you been up to?" Mike asked as he continued to hit the cigarillo.

"Nothing. Just peeping the scene," Shawn replied. He stood back, watched, and waited until Mike passed him the blunt back.

"You heard 'bout that dude, Fat, didn't you?" Shawn wanted to know.

"No. What he do this time?" Mike asked.

"Would you believe, that dude done robbed the gas station up the street."

"For real?" Mike passed Shawn the blunt.

"I heard that boy snort dope now," Shawn said.

"I don't know how true that is, though," Mike responded.

"Man, I remember when we were young, he said he would never put a finger on a drug," Shawn reminisced.

"Well, people grow up and change, my brotha." Mike lowered his voice, as they saw Fat walking up the street.

"Wut up wit' it, y'all!"

"What it do?" Fat said.

"Nothing," Mike and Shawn said in unison.

"Brothas just struggling out here. People don't have no money living in the hood, man," Mike added."

"I know. That's true. But guess what? I just hit a good ass lic last night, ya dig?" Fat said.

"I heard," responded Shawn.

"How you know?" Fat wanted to know.

"You know how the boys around the hood talk," Mike said, laughing from his high. Man I heard you robbed the gas station.

"You better be happy you didn't get caught, though," Shawn added, laughing at himself 'cause he thought his words were so funny, being high and all.

"I know," Fat said. He started to walk away. "I didn't rob the place. I just took some beer and stuff. Well, I'll see y'all a lil' later, then. Folks stay up and stay safe," he hollered as he walked off.

Mike and Shawn began walking down the street toward Shawn's house. "You wanna get on the computer?" Shawn wanted to know.

"Yeah, 'cause on MySpace I got, like, five hundred friends," Mike said proudly.

They walked into the house and saw Shawn's mother, Lisa.

"Hey, Mom," Shawn said. He kept his distance from her so that she wouldn't smell the weed on his clothing.

"Hey, baby boy."

"Hey, Ms. Lisa." Mike spoke to his friend's mother in a polite and respectful way. He knew that if he wanted to hang around Shawn, he had to come correct, because Ms. Lisa was all about business and wanted the same for her son.

"We gonna hit up the computer," Shawn told his mom.

As the boys walked toward Shawn's room, Lisa reminded them about the dangers of the computer.

"Shawn, don't be in there chatting and messing around in places on that Internet you know you ain't got no business being."

"I got you, Ma."

"Listen, boy! Too much stuff happening on that chat line. Be careful, and don't be putting your business out there. You better not even chat. It is dangerous. People are crazy nowadays."

"Ma, I know. You only remind me one hundred times a day. But like I said, I got this!"

Mike and Shawn booted the computer and chatted while they waited to find their site.

Mike Johnson was sixteen years old and the only child of his mother, Diane. He had never met his father and finally stopped asking about him after realizing he would never get that pleasure. Mike was a tall, good-looking young man with oak-brown skin and chestnut eyes. In school he was an average student, popular with the girls, and he played basketball. Even though he was six feet tall, he was not a strong player, but he still looked impressive. He really didn't care about school, though. He was more into the girls and smoking a little weed every now and then. He was into clothes, too, but he could not always afford them. He went to school to look good and to catch the ladies' eyes. He missed a lot of days after his mom lost her job due to a huge layoff at the factory.

Shawn Williams was as different from Mike as a dog is from a cat. He was a spoiled teen. His mother, Lisa, cherished him. All her life she'd wanted a son, so when he was born he was her one and only love. She lived and breathed for her child. Shawn stood 5'8", and he was a good student. Most of the time he received A's and B's in class, and he planned on going to college. Actually, he had already selected the college. He was going to the same school his mother had graduated from, the University of Arkansas at Pine Bluff, and he had already received his acceptance letter. Shawn couldn't wait to go. He loved girls as much as the next fellow, but he knew that his mother had high hopes for him, and he wanted to be successful. Though Shawn's parents were divorced, they both spent much time nurturing and loving their child.

Shawn was a handsome boy with brown eyes. He was somewhat muscular, as he hooped on the block after school with the other neighborhood fellas on the regular. He was also a computer wiz, self-taught, and he could maneuver the web sites with complete ease.

Finally the computer came on. Shawn typed in his e-mail address and password, and his page came up immediately. He had one hundred messages, all from the same person. It was a person they had been chatting with for a while, a teenage girl named Sylvia, who said she was from the same area as them. She'd introduced them to her cousin online, and they were all just friends. Sylvia seemed like a nice person. They had never met her, but planned to do so soon. She promised that at that time she would date one of the guys. In the meantime, they chatted about everything that was happening in the world, including drugs, sex and music.

Before he turned off the computer an instant message popped up.

"What's up son? Shawn's dad asked.

"Nothing much. Just surfing the net. What's up with you?

"Just trying to prepare myself for school."

"I'm proud of your son."

"Thanks dad."

"If you need anything, let me know."

"I will dad."

"I'll check with you later."

"See ya!"

CHAPTER 2

Throw Them Hands

The next day, Mike awoke to the bright sun peeking through his window. He looked at his alarm clock, which displayed 6:00 a.m. *Oh great! Another day at school,* he said to himself. He got up and sorted out his clothes, then laid them across the chair in his room. He walked over to his closet and looked for a pair of shoes. None suited him. They were getting old and out of style. They were all over six months old, which was too old for him to be sportin'. This pissed him off, because he didn't want to deal with folk's joning him about his shoes. He dreaded going to school in his old gear, but decided to just deal with it. He hopped in and out of the shower, said 'bye to his mother, and off he went.

Mike wasn't too anxious to get to school. Every time he arrived, someone had something to say about his clothes. Today he told himself that he wasn't going to take it. He was fed up with it. Plus, he only had a few weeks left in summer school before he could enjoy the rest of the season. He was going to summer school because he'd failed English, and he had to do it over if he wanted to pass to eleventh grade.

Mike was sitting in class when a boy just burst out, "Y'all seen them new J's that came out Saturday? Them mugs fresh!" The whole class began to talk about the new shoes. Mike felt left out because he couldn't afford those kinds of shoes, so he just sat there quietly. He felt really out of place.

Mike hated school. It was supposed to be about learning, but it was really a fashion show. All you would see were kids wearing J's, Bathing Apes, Forces, and Tim's. He hated that his mother had gotten laid off. Plus, most of the time he couldn't get that kind of wear, anyway, because it was just too expensive. He couldn't wait until he got some money to buy that kind of stuff. He needed some money quick and fast.

"Wut up, Mike! Boy, isn't it time for some new shoes?" a classmate asked with a funny tone, looking down at Mike's feet. The class was over, and they were in the hallway.

"What you say?" Mike was furious. Who the heck did this dude think he was, walking up on him and talking down about his gear?

"Nigga, you heard what I said," the boy replied.

Mike swung at him. He hit the boy with a powerful blow to his face that knocked him to the ground. "You ain't talking now, punk," Mike taunted.

Several teens lingering in the hall ran to get the principal. Once the principal arrived, he escorted Mike and the other young man to his office. After he determined what had happened, he suspended Mike for five days.

Mike was so worried. He knew his mother was going to be angry. *Man, what am I going to tell my mother when I get home? She gonna be real mad at me*, he thought. As he was leaving school, he decided to go by Shawn's house.

Mike was in summer school, and Shawn was at home, waiting to attend his first year of college. Mike knew that Shawn was at home smoking his life away.

Shawn was miserable. He wasn't pleased with his life. He'd grown up as an only child, and his mom and dad had recently divorced. Their divorce really affected him. He smoked so much because he was so depressed. At one point, he was going to kill himself because he was so stressed out. His mom seemed as if she didn't want him anymore. She stopped buying food for him and left him on his own most of the time. He had a job, but he quit. He didn't do much of anything except smoke and chat on his computer.

Shawn was an above-average student much of the time and had already began taking college courses while in the twelfth grade. He couldn't wait until he finally left for college. He had eight weeks left before heading to the south. They say time changes things and that was true. Shawn became a stronger and more confident person after his dad reconnected with him.

Mike changed his mind about going to visit Shawn. Instead, he continued walking home. When he got there, his mother wanted to know why he was at home so early. She was angry.

"Mike, what is your problem?" She walked up on him like she was about to knock him out.

"I got put out for fighting."

"What! Why did that happen?"

"Some dude was joning on me, talking about my shoes. So I had to throw them hands."

"Boy, are you crazy? Here I am unemployed and can't find a job, yet you are messing up an opportunity to do better. You are messing up your life. Now what? You got put out of summer school. What's gonna happen now?"

"I go back after five days. I'll pass my class."

"You better!"

Mike's mom, Diane, was a nice woman in her early thirties with a caramel complexion. She'd had Mike when she was seventeen years old. Diane worked hard to put food on the table. Now she was receiving unemployment and trying to find another job.

"Mike, I told you about concerning yourself with what others say about you. The same boys you see running around here with these high-priced shoes are going to be nothing in life, cause 'the man' make the shoes. See, you been through a struggle, so you are going to get what you want, 'cause you are hungry for it. Son, what I mean is this: you will work harder for success, because you can't have these nice things now. When you can get them, you will appreciate them more than the kids who don't have to work so hard. You can't help the way you live. I work very hard to put food on the table for you. I'm sorry I can't afford all those high-priced shoes for you, but I'm doing what I can. I don't want you out there selling drugs and things. That's not good money. I don't wanna wake up and hear you have been killed."

"That's not going to happen to me. I'm a man. I can fight."

"But you can't fight those guns, though."

"Alright, Momma. I'm going to Shawn's, okay?"

"Don't let the streetlight catch you."

Mike looked at her with a funny expression. Then he went outside and headed to Shawn's house. As he was walking, he saw all the street hustlers on the corner making money. It made him want to get out there. When he arrived at Shawn's, he found him sitting at the computer.

"Hi, Ms. Lisa," Mike said in his Wally voice from the "Leave It to Beaver" television show.

"Hey, Mike! How are you doing today?"

"I'm doing good."

Lisa was a thirty-five-year-old school teacher at the local high school, where she taught fifth-grade students. She was pretty friendly with Shawn's friends, but Shawn had said she was becoming withdrawn ever since the divorce. That was too bad, because Lisa was fione.

"Shawn, I'm gone," Lisa hollered as she walked out the door for her tutoring sessions at the community center.

"Wut up man! You wanna hit this blunt?" Shawn asked.

"Yeah," Mike replied.

After a few minutes of passing the blunt back and forth, they were so high they were numb. They got on MySpace and started chatting.

"Man, you see that fine gal right there? That's Sylvia. She posted some more pictures."

"Let's chat with her," Shawn said.

"Let's do it!" Mike agreed.

While they talked to Sylvia, she told them she was having a party and she wanted them to come see her. Since they were so high, they asked her for her address, and without even knowing who she really was, they went to the party.

This was what Lisa was trying so hard to tell them. She had told the boys that people on the Internet were often not who they claimed to be, and that they had to be careful. But the teenagers ignored the warning and did what they wanted to do. Disobedience makes for a hard head.

They had to take a bus to Sylvia's house. The address she gave them was in a bad neighborhood. They got off the bus and began walking toward the girl's house, when all of a sudden a boy came up and put a gun to Shawn's head.

"Give me everything in your damn pocket!"

"Alright, man. Just don't kill me," Shawn pleaded. The silver forty-five was pressed against his temple.

"You, too, boy! Empty the pockets, Gee."

"Here, man," Mike said.

Then the boy ran. Immediately, Mike and Shawn realized they had been set up. Luckily, they still had their bus transfers. They went back home, unable to believe it. They'd been robbed!

"Man, I'm not going on MySpace no more," Mike said angrily.

"Me, neither," Shawn said, shaking his head.

"Man, let's smoke another blunt." Shawn rolled a strawberry cigarillo.

"Hell, yeah," Mike replied. "I'm glad you didn't bring that weed with you," he laughed.

"Me, too. This whole quarter would have been gone," Shawn said.

As they walked and smoked, they saw the bus and waved it down. Once it stopped, they got on.

"Shawn, I need to come up."

On the ride home, they talked about the need to make money.

"Yeah, it's really hard in the hood." They got off the bus and walked out into the streets near Shawn's house.

"These dudes out here making money. I got to get on the grind and hustle," Mike said as he pulled on the cigarillo. "I can do that for a lil' while. You know, to get a lil' change."

"Man, you can do whatever you want to do. You know I got your back. But man, hustling drugs ain't nothing but trouble," Shawn told him.

"And I got your back, too."

Since they were both high and had just been robbed, their mind wasn't right. They continued to walk the hood.

"Hey, you wanna walk to the store?" Mike inquired.

"No doubt."

As they walked, they saw an old friend hustling. "Man, everybody making money," Mike said.

When they got back to Shawn's house, Mike decided to remove his MySpace page. Then an ad popped up. It read, *HEY! YOU WANNA MAKE SOME MONEY? CLICK HERE!* So Mike clicked it.

"Man, you hardheaded! We just got set up cause of this crap!" Shawn tried hard to reason with his boy.

"I know, but this sounds like a good offer. I'm going to try it," Mike said excitedly.

"Alright. I told you, I always got your back." But Shawn was worried.

When Mike clicked the ad, it led them to a man named George. He was a local man from the same city they lived in. He said that he had a profitable business and needed to hire some good workers. George told Mike to meet him at 74th Street so that he could give him the information in person. Mike agreed to do so the following day.

CHAPTER 3

Struggle No More

The next day, Mike and Shawn walked down to 74th Street, where they had promised to meet George. As they walked, they saw big, tight cars riding on twenty-fours and drug dealers slinging their stash on the street corners. Mike was easily impressed. He got so excited watching the bling-bling that the dealers were frontin' for people to see.

"Man, did you see that blue Chevy Caprice?" he asked, as he gestured expressively with his hands.

"Yeah, man! That was tight."

Mike wished he had one. Somehow, the hunger in his eyes worried Shawn. Shawn warned his friend, "Man, you better not be out here in these streets, 'cause once I get to college there is not going to be anyone out here to watch out for you, ya dig? These dudes are all about making their own money, and they would do anything in their power to eliminate you. Ya hear me, Mike?

"I know. I'ma be careful, bro'. I know it's not safe in the hood. But I gotta do what I gotta do."

"How do we know it's not another setup?" Shawn wanted to know.

"Man, don't worry about that. If it is a setup, I got this for them."

Mike reached down into his waistband and pulled out a silver forty-five.

"Man, where did you get that from? And don't point that over here!"

"Don't worry about that. I got connections out here in these streets. The less you know, the better. I got this, dawg."

"Is it loaded?" Shawn asked.

"Nope."

"Then why are you bringing it out?

"To scare them or pistol-whip them," Mike said.

"Where did you get it from?"

"From my cousin Tony. You know Tony, don't you?"

"I didn't know that he would give you a gun.

Did you pay for it?"

"Nope. Why?"

"As much as you like clothes, I know you would have copped a few outfits first if you had some money."

"True that!

"Dude, just be careful with that. And be careful who you show it to, 'cause the cops would holla at you in a bad way."

Mike put the gun back in his waistband, and the boys proceeded toward their destination. As they approached the spot they'd been told to go to, they realized that a man was standing in the door of a vacant house, waiting for their presence.

"Wut up, boy? What ya name?" the man asked.

"Mike."

"What, you don't have a last name?"

"Oh, yeah. Mike Johnson."

"Whose old dude wit' ya?"

"My name is Shawn."

"Well, my name is George Deavers." George continued with his round of questions. "What school do y'all go to?"

"I go to Washington Heights High School," Mike said.

"I leave for college later this summer," Shawn added.

"I just wanna know who I am dealing with. I already know who applied for this job," George said with a hearty laugh. "You boys ever worked before?"

"No, I haven't," Mike said, hoping this wouldn't hurt his chances of getting a job.

"You boys know this is a grown man's job?" George asked. "You do know what kind of job this is, don't you?"

"Not really," they said in unison.

"Y'all are delivery boys. You deliver what I give you." When George looked Mike directly in the eyes, his happy, friendly demeanor changed.

"I want you to get this package off for me," he said in a low voice.

"You mean, get on da block?" Shawn asked.

"Yeah." George touched his gun. "Y'all ain't got no problem

with that, now, do you?"

"I can do that," Mike said. "I thought this was a real job, though."

"It is real. You get paid for doing the work."

"Okay. I'ma do this."

"Not me, man. Not my gig." Shawn turned to walk away, but then he stopped. "Mike, man, you sure you wanna do this?"

"Hell, yeah!"

"I best be able to trust you," George said. "I want you to start tonight."

"Alright," Mike said. As the boys walked away, a man approached them.

"Wut up! My name is Jeff. Here is your product. You got to get this off tonight. We expect eight hundred dollars in the morning."

"Eight hundred dollars!" Shawn yelled.

"Yeah. Your take is four hundred dollars," Jeff said with a cheesy smile.

"That's a deal. I'm down." Mike was excited to be paid four hundred for one night's work. He had never, ever seen that much money all at one time. "So all I have to do is get this off and I will get four hundred dollars?" he repeated, to be sure of what he had heard.

"Yeah, "Jeff replied.

They parted ways, with the reminder from Jeff that Mike was to meet him back at the same spot in the morning.

Shawn went home, because it was not his intention to become involved in the drug trade. But Mike went to make that dough. He set up his post to get his clientele up.

Mike was selling pretty well throughout the night, until he heard someone screaming at him.

"What you doing? Get off my block!" a boy yelled from behind him.

"Man, forget you! I'm not going nowhere," Mike shouted back.

"Man, get up or I'm going to get you up," the boy said.

"Well, you are just going to have to get me up, then," Mike said with confidence.

The dude walked up on Mike and tried to take him, but Mike hit the boy in the stomach so hard that he threw up blood. Then the boy ran. Mike stayed there and collected his eight hundred dollars. He felt like the king of the hood.

Mike returned to summer school when his suspension for fighting was finally over. He did his course work, completed the rest of summer school, and passed to the next grade. Meanwhile, he stayed at his post and continued to rake in the dollars.

Shawn attended college, all the way in Arkansas. He felt alone there. He didn't have anyone to talk to, no one to relate to. All he had was the Internet. He often went online to MySpace. There he met a lot of people, but most importantly he met a girl named Julia. She said she was eighteen years of age and lived close by. He told her that he felt alone because everybody at school was two-faced. He couldn't trust them. She told him to leave school for the weekend and come meet her. Shawn said he would think about it but he decided not to, since he didn't know the girl, anyway.

After two months went by, Shawn realized he hadn't heard from Mike. He decided to call him.

"Wut it do, man?" Shawn asked.

"Nothing, man. Just getting my money. I'm living it up right now, man, like I told you. I got, like, two stacks put up for me, man. I could do this for the rest of my life, man," Mike said.

"What does your mom think of this? Does she know?" Shawn asked.

"Moms don't even know. She thinks I'm at school. I stopped going to school. You know, I'm not going back."

Shawn asked, "Man, that money can't be that good?"

"Oh, dawg, yeah, it is. When you come back up here, I got something stashed away for you, dawg. You holla. I gotta get back to da block," Mike said.

"Later, dude. Keep your stash for yourself, man. I'm not getting my hands dirty."

"No problem, dude. I'll holla later. I got a sell to make, a'ight."

CHAPTER 4

Through with the Game

When they hung up the phone, Shawn couldn't stop thinking about what Mike had stashed away for him. Eventually, he got on MySpace to talk to Julia. Shawn felt alone, even though he had everything a person could have ever wanted and more. He liked being in the hood, but felt rejected when people outside of the hood disrespected him. To them, he talked funny because he had that northern dialect, but to him, the folks in the south were the ones who couldn't talk. They had that long drawl.

Over the next three weeks, Shawn worried so much about Mike that his grades began to slip. Julia convinced him to seek tutoring, which he did. Julia was turning out to be a positive influence on him, even though he did not know her. She was just a MySpace pal.

****

One Tuesday night, Mike was hustling on the corner when a car rolled up behind him and shot him in the leg.

"Dude, you remember when you hit me?" the boy in the car said.

"What!" Mike screamed, grabbing his leg and trying to find cover.

The boy answered with another shot, which hit Mike in the leg and foot. Mike ran, but he didn't get far before he fell to the ground. As he reached to pull his own gun out, a local man ran to help.

"You alright?"

"No, man! Call the police. I have been shot," Mike yelled. The pain was so excruciating. It was worse than any pain Mike had ever felt before.

The man tried to keep Mike conscious by asking him questions. "What's your home phone number?"

Mike whispered weakly, "213-7727."

The man called an ambulance and Mike's mother. "Hello. Is this Mike's mother?" the man asked.

"Yes, this is she," Diane said in her sweet, angelic voice.

"Your son has been shot, but not badly, only in the leg. The paramedics are putting him into the ambulance. They are taking him to the Kenneth Hall Hospital."

"Oh, my God!" Diane said tearfully. She quickly hung up the phone and rushed to the hospital. When she got there, she saw her son lying in the hospital bed.

"I'm sorry, Mom," Mike said.

"Sshh, baby. I'm so happy you are alive. Get your rest. We'll talk tomorrow."

Diane immediately called Shawn to tell him about Mike. Shawn was sad, because he had always told his friend that he had his back and would always be there for him. He felt he had failed his friend. He told Diane that he was sorry to hear such bad news and would come back to see Mike in a few days. Shawn was glad that he'd chosen college instead of the streets. Now he was more determined than ever to talk his friend out of the drug game.

The next day, Mike was lying in the hospital bed all sad and blue when his mother walked in.

"Mom, I'm sorry for disobeying you."

"I talked to the school this morning and they said you haven't been there. You stopped going to school, boy!" she screamed.

"Yeah, I meant to tell you."

"What?" Diane said angrily.

"I have been selling drugs for the entire summer," he said.

"What? I'm not going to even get mad at you. The bullets in your leg and foot should be the warning you need to change your life now. I hope that you have learned your lesson."

"I have. I just wanted to do it for a lil' while, Mom," Mike cried. "I didn't mean for it to go to this extreme."

"Didn't I tell you, you couldn't fight guns? You didn't listen. Look what you got yourself into!"

"I'm through with the game, Mom."

CHAPTER 5

The Return

When Mike was on his way back home, he saw Shawn walking down the street toward his house which was only a short block down. He told his mom to stop the car, so he could tell him to stop by his house. When they arrived home, Shawn ran fast arriving at the same time as Mike and his mother. He helped Mike get out the car.

"Man, you aren't going back out there, are you?" Shawn wanted to know.

"Man, I don't know. I might, 'cause that money was beautiful. I told my mom I wasn't, but I really don't know. I think I might."

"Man, don't go back out there! Next time, you might get killed."

"Man, school ain't for me. Just because you a college boy now, you think you better than me," Mike said angrily.

"Man, I'm just telling you what could happen to you. You better open your ears and listen to me, cause them other dudes on the street out on da block ain't gone tell you this. They don't care about you. They trying to get money just like you."

"I can't wait till your ass goes back to college, so I won't see your lame ass no more."

"What! That's just gravy with me. At least I'm going to make something out of myself. I'm gone, dude."

"Step then, punk!"

****

Mike was at home, letting his leg heal. His tutor visited him every day. Diane encouraged the school administrators to allow her son to return to school. She also insisted they give her son a tutor.

"How's everything going?" Diane asked as she brought him a glass of cold orange juice.

"Everything's going good, Ma."

"Here, drink this glass of juice." Diane passed it to him.

"Thanks."

"You can go back to school next month. You ready to go back?" she asked.

"No, not really."

"But you will go back to school."

As Diane sat with Mike, she couldn't help but notice all the different shoes and clothes he had in his room. "Mike, you made this much money out there?" Diane asked.

"I made good money."

Diane just shook her head. She felt bad that she had been so busy with her own life she didn't notice what her own son was doing. She realized she would have to pay more attention to him.

****

Mike went back to school. He was doing well, but he missed da block. He missed making quick and easy money. He wanted to get back out there, but he'd promised his mom he wouldn't do so.

"Hey, how was school today?" Diane asked.

"It was all good," Mike replied as he walked to the family room. He got on the computer and went to MySpace. He wanted to talk to George. Mike told George that he would return very soon, but George told him that he would have to return in two days, because he had a customer who was going to pay one thousand dollars for a product. Mike agreed.

CHAPTER 6

A Hardhead Makes a Soft Ass

In two days, Mike was back on da block–the same one he got shot on.

"Wut up, man?" a man in a blue Chevy Caprice asked him.

"Nothing. Just trying to make money."

"That's right," the man said. He gave Mike the money, took the product from him, and drove away.

About five minutes later, Mike saw the Caprice circle around the corner and come back. He didn't know what to do. He didn't know whether to run or to stay. The man got out the car and held Mike up at gunpoint. "Give me all the shit you got!"

"A'ight, man! Here, here's everything," Mike said in a nervous voice. Then the man took off.

Mike was so scared he didn't know what to do. He couldn't tell George, 'cause he would probably try to kill him. Mike went home and started panicking. He walked around in circles. He knew that his life was on the line. The man had robbed him for one thousand dollars in product and two thousand dollars in cash, so the robber's total take was three thousand dollars.

Mike got on the computer and nervously sent George a message. He told him that he'd been robbed for everything. George sent a message back stating that if Mike didn't get the money to him by next week, it would be a problem.

Mike didn't know what to do. He had only had one grand left, which he stashed away. He couldn't ask his mom, because he'd promised her, plus he knew she didn't have the money. So he took the matter into his own hands and went out to buy a gun from Fat down the street. He was planning on robbing the local gas station. He didn't know what else to do. He was stuck and scared. His life was on the line.

At 6 p.m., Diane came home. "Hey, how was school?" she asked.

"Good. We didn't have any homework today. I'm going to walk down the street to get something to snack on from the gas station. You want something?"

"No, but thanks for asking."

When Mike walked out the house, he thought every car he saw was someone George sent to kill him or something. As he was getting closer to the station, he saw four dudes already robbing the store. Gunshots came from every direction. Mike got on the ground. People were running everywhere. His life was in danger again. He was frightened. As he lay on the ground, he prayed to God to help him. "Please, God, help me! Please save me from myself." Mike lay on the ground for the longest time.

Diane was watching TV when the program was interrupted with a breaking news report. "I'm Catherine Davis with Channel Five. We have a breaking news report that a local gas station has been robbed. Three teens were found dead and four people are wounded. We'll report more as more information becomes available."

Diane suddenly remembered her son saying that he was going to the gas station, and she realized he hadn't returned yet. She totally panicked and began to pray out loud,

"Please, God, let my son be okay! Please, Lord!"

As she sat there and continued to think about her son, the news came back on. At the same time, her doorbell rang. She ran to answer it and saw that it was the police. Then the news repeated the names of the dead teens. "The three dead teens have been identified. They are John Davis, Corey Taylor, and Michael Williams."

Diane fell to her knees, screaming. The policemen tried to comfort her, but couldn't. They called for an ambulance, because she would need to be sedated.

"My son, Lord! Not my son! Please let it be a mistake, Lord. Oh please, God, help me!"

Her screams were deafening.

CHAPTER 7

The Funeral

Everyone was contacted about Mike's death. The police reported that Mike was an innocent bystander who was shot while walking to the gas station. However, they did say he had a gun in his pocket. But he was never in the store and did not even know the guys who robbed the store. He was heading to the wrong place at the wrong time.

Shawn took his friend's death extremely hard. They had argued the last time they saw each other. Shawn had tried to convince his friend to get out of the game, but to no avail. He flew home to be with his family and attend the funeral.

Diane asked Shawn to be on program at the funeral. She knew that her son had respected and looked up to his best friend. But Shawn had one thing he had to do first. He called his dad and discussed what happened. His dad gave him so much confidence, so Shawn went to a phone booth and called and reported the drug dealer. He found a pay phone that you could use to report drug activity without getting involved, and he reported George. He told the police how George used the Internet and MySpace to recruit teens to sell for him. He explained how he paid them good money to keep them in the game.

The police department had a sting and busted George and his workers. They found out that George was responsible for the man who'd robbed Mike, and for other crimes in the neighborhood. That was how he kept his boys in the game. He gave them the product and sent another worker out to buy it. This worker would rob the seller, and then the seller would be forced to repay George. It was a slick game to keep people under his wing, because they could never repay the money that was stolen. This way, he kept them on da block in his click.

****

As Shawn was walking down the street, he saw those big fancy cars that Mike always talked about when they used to walk together. It made him think about the good times. As he approached Mike's street, he saw Fat.

"Man, I heard about what happened to your boy. Man, sorry to hear about that."

"Thanks, man."

"I saw that dude the same day he died."

Shawn walked to Mike's mother's house. The house was packed with all her relatives.

"Hey, Shawn," Diane said as she let him in. "I'm glad you could come."

"There was no way I would miss being here. He was my best friend. I just wanna say I'm sorry." He hugged her. Then he left.

As Shawn walked back home, he thought about what Mike used to say to him all the time when they were walking down the street. He used to say, "Fellas out here are struggling. We need to get out here and get that paper."

****

On Monday, December 1, Shawn was dressing for the funeral when his mother came in and asked, "Shawn, are you alright?"

"Yeah, I'm alright. Just feeling a little sick inside. I didn't even get a speech prepared for this. I'm just going to speak from the heart," Shawn said.

"That would be good," Lisa said.

"I will be ready in a few minutes," Shawn said.

As they pulled up to the church, Shawn saw many of Mike's friends and family members whom he hadn't seen in a long time. He took a seat in the back row and waited until it was time to say his remarks. When they called his name, he walked up real slowly and nervously.

"How's everybody doing?" The people smiled.

"Today is a real sad day for me, the day I have to bury my best friend." Tears started rolling down Shawn's face. He looked down at the cream-colored casket. "I really don't have a speech prepared for today, so I'm going to speak from my heart. I remember the times Mike and I used to talk about what we were going to do when we got older. He used to always say, 'Man, I'm going to get out of here and move to a better place.' I used to think he was joking and playing, but he was serious. Mike gave me the inspiration to do better things, 'cause he wanted to be so successful. No matter how hard the struggle, he wanted to achieve it but, he just didn't do the things he needed to do to obtain success. I always wanted to be like him because he wanted a better life. Yes, believe it or not, I did. You see, Mike had the determination to do things even though they were the wrong things to do. The problem was, he didn't follow the right directions to get to the dream he wanted. Everybody knows that Mike wanted to make a lot of money. But all money is not good money. His path should have been to stay in school, become educated and work hard for an honest income. Also, Mike needed to have friends who wanted the same things but who was willing to do the right thing to get what they desired.

You can't be successful without positive people in your life. You have to keep praying and keep doing what you can to have a better life. At first, he was on the right path by doing all he could to finish school; even going to summer school, but he still struggled to do the right thing. In the end, he chose the wrong way to get ahead. Today, I wanna say thanks. Thanks for everything. Thanks for being there when I needed a friend. No, a brother! You are so slick, Mike. You said you were going to a better place, and you did. I'm going to miss you, my friend. I'll see you again someday. We'll holla again. Later, dude. I love you. I'm going to be successful for both of us, man. I'm going to miss you, man." Shawn walked away from the podium.

CHAPTER 8

In His Name

Shawn returned to college with a heavy heart. He decided he would find a place to mentor teenagers. They needed to have positive guidance in their lives. If they lacked positive influences, it would be easy for the negative faction to get to them. He wanted them to understand that easy money was not good money, and that with fast cash came much pain.

Shawn went to the Boys Club in Arkansas and talked to the director about starting up a program for college students to mentor boys from ages eight to sixteen. The goals of the program would be to teach kids to say no and to train them in a sport so that they would have things to do.

The director was impressed with the young man. She liked his ideas. He would recruit college students to work with the boys. They would have rap sessions and discussions. They would invite successful men, rap stars and basketball players, to talk to the group about the dangers of drugs and getting involved with the wrong people. They would also teach them how to look for a job and interview for positions, and talk to them about the perils of making bad decisions. Finally, they would take field trips to local jails, to let the boys see the real deal about being locked up with no way out.

Shawn was so excited about the program. He named the program The M.I.K.E. Project. It stood for Making Individuals Knowledgeable Entirely.

The program excelled and became a great hit. One day, a young lady called the center to interview the people responsible for the program. The director told her what time the young man who'd started the program would be there with the kids, and the young lady agreed to come at that time.

On Monday, February 10, Shawn arrived at the center with the rest of the volunteers. They were excited to have the newspaper interested in their story. This would be a great way to get additional donations to support the field trips and the incentive gifts that they gave the students for participating in the program.

When the director of the program, Ms. Sheppard, introduced Shawn to the reporter, he smiled.

"This is Julia Simmons," the director said. "Julia, this is Shawn Williams."

They both smiled. It was the Julia he had been corresponding with on the Internet, the one who had encouraged him to stay in school and make something out of his life. She was interning at the newspaper while majoring in journalism at her college.

After the interview, Shawn and Julia went to dinner. It was a good time for Shawn. After all, he had found the girl who made his heart pound.

Shawn wished that his friend could have lived to see what life had to offer. With a little hard work in class and the right attitude, you could achieve anything.

Shawn knew from listening to his teachers and his parents that when you get involved in drugs, there are only three things you can expect: jail, hospitalization or death. Why would anyone want those kinds of choices when you can choose jobs like computer programming, teaching, becoming a doctor, a lawyer, a mechanic, or anything else your mind could dream of?

Shawn also wanted to spread the message about the dangers of the Internet. Even though he met Julia online, he never set a time to meet her, because she could have been a murderer or someone who planned to do horrible things to him. He just used her as a sounding board, never sharing his personal information. He would never again meet a stranger the way he and Mike had. Yes, it was nice to finally meet Julia and find out that she was a nice person. But he had still been very smart about chatting with her.

Shawn learned one important thing. He learned that his inner voice was right when it told him to be strong and persevere. We all have this same positive inner voice that tries to lead us in the right direction. We just have to be willing to listen. Don't let your negative voice win. Shawn's positive inner voice wants everyone to always remember, "We may all have a little hood in us, but we don't have to always represent the hood in a negative way. Even the hood has positive people, if you just let them shine."

The Price of Disobedience

CHAPTER ONE

Getting Ready for the Weekend

"Hey girl, are you coming over for the weekend?" Alexis asked her cousin Demetra.

"If I get the weekend off from my job, I'll definitely come over."

"Girl, my dad is not going to be home because he has to go to Washington, D.C., for a business trip."

"That's cool, girl! I'll call you on Thursday to let you know. Plus, girl, I want to show you something on the Internet," Demetra said with a giggle.

"My dad bought some new computer supplies and he has speakers and everything. Do you know how to attach them?"

Demetra laughed again. "You are so silly! I can do anything with a computer. I'll teach you this weekend."

"Okay, cuz. Call me. Bye."

"Bye, silly girl."

Alexis Kirby was the thirteen-year-old daughter of Harrison and Janice Kirby. She was their only child, and as such she owned many technical toys, designer clothes and other trinkets that she didn't mind sharing with her older cousin Demetra.

Soft-spoken and shy, Alexis always looked forward to seeing her cousin. They had spent many weekends together, as Demetra was Janice's favorite niece. Alexis was a petite, beautiful child. She was 4'11" and weighed ninety pounds soaking wet. She had the most beautiful little physique. She was built like a coke bottle, with all those little curves in the right places, so much so that her parents forbade her to wear clothes that showed too much skin and made her seem older than she actually was. Her shoulder-length hair was so soft and bouncy that to maintain it she wore braids.

In addition to being as cute as a little doll, she had the most beautiful bright eyes, which always caught the attention of others. Her mother had shared many stories of photographers and so-called agents asking that little Alexis be brought to their studio for pictures and auditions for commercials. Her parents wanted their only child to become educated and start her own business, rather than spend long hours prancing around the world auditioning for commercials and modeling assignments that she might never book.

Little, brown-eyed Alexis was a dream daughter, what parents call a good child. She was clean and neat and treated her clothes and expensive things with pride. She never gave her parents' one ounce of trouble, so her parents believed that she was responsible and not easily led. She was obedient. She studied and completed her homework without problems and attended church regularly. As a matter of fact, her parents were faithful members of a local church because even if they tried to miss a Sabbath, Alexis would prod and beg until all were dressed and sitting like the perfect family in their late-model Mercedes on their way to church.

Demetra was the only daughter of Casey Sylvester. She had two brothers, one who was two years older than she was and one six years younger. Being a middle child, she felt like she didn't get the attention that she often craved.

It was either her brother John getting into trouble or her baby brother, Adam, soaking up all the attention with his big hazel eyes. In addition, it didn't help that her mother had finally married her long-term boyfriend, who preferred Adam, his own son. So Demetra worked on gaining the affections of her Aunt Janice and Uncle Harrison.

Whatever Demetra wanted, Aunt Janice and Uncle Harrison would get it for her if they could. They treated her as if she was their other daughter, giving her unconditional love, trust and access to their young daughter. They believed that Alexis needed an older sister or cousin to share her secrets with and seek support from, especially since she was so shy. They had long found that Alexis had a difficult time sharing her problems and concerns with her parents, because she didn't want to change how they felt about her.

****

To assure that their child was safe from predators and others who might want to do her harm, the Kirby's educated her about sexual predators. They read stories to her and watched movies about children being abducted. They took her to plays with similar themes, had several police officers talk to her and her friends before birthday parties, and even put parent controls on the Internet, after fully explaining the dangers of high technology and Internet surfing. They were sure that they had done everything to protect their child, short of assigning her a big, bald, muscular, gun-toting bodyguard. Little did they know that the apple of their eye would fall prey to the very person they invited into their home to spend countless hours with their child.

CHAPTER 2

Slow Your Roll

The phone rang at the Kirby's house at six a.m. on Thursday.

"Hey, girl," Alexis answered the phone with sleep still in her eyes.

It was Demetra. "You getting ready for school?"

"Not until six-thirty. My alarm is set and I am going back to sleep. Are you coming over?"

"Yeah, girl. You still have your digital camera?"

"That's Momma's camera. I'm sure it is here. What do we need that for?"

"Gurl, we gon' post our pictures on the Internet," said Demetra.

"Girl, you are so crazy! Nope, I am not doing that. That's dangerous."

"Then we will post some fake pictures up."

"Why are we posting pictures, anyway?"

"Wait 'til I get there and I'll explain then. I'll see you tomorrow. Don't forget to bake me a cake."

"Okay. You always want me to bake you a cake, but this is the last time."

"Yeah, right, big head. See you later. Bye."

"Bye, gurl."

Alexis laid her head back on her pillow and slept for an additional twenty minutes. Then she got up, took her shower and put on her clothes. After eating a bowl of cereal, she went to inform her mother that she was getting ready to leave to catch the school bus that stopped three doors from her house.

She was looking forward to seeing her cousin. Whenever they were together, they had so much fun. Plus, her cousin was beautiful and had lots of male friends, and they would talk into the wee hours of the night on the phone with them. Even though she was not supposed to date, Alexis talked regularly on the phone to boys Demetra had introduced her to. She never met them, but enjoyed talking and laughing on the phone and, best of all, pretending to be all of sixteen years old.

As she shook her mother awake, she said, "Mom, Demetra is coming tomorrow and needs you to pick her up at six p.m. at the Metro Link."

"Alright. Let me get up and get ready for work. Are you leaving this minute?"

"Yes. I have three minutes before the bus comes."

"Come straight home, and no company."

"I know. You tell me that every day."

"I'll be here around seven p.m. tonight. I have a late meeting. Eat a pizza from the freezer and I'll bring you some Burger King or something later."

"See you," Alexis called out as she rushed to the bus stop.

****

All day at school, Alexis thought about what they would do over the weekend. Rather than keep her mind on her studies, she jotted down things to do when she got home. First she would contact Jamestown's movie theater to check on what movies would be playing and the times. Then she would call Demetra to give her the information, and hopefully this boy, Gary, who she had been talking on the phone with, would be able to come to St. Louis and meet them at the movie. He sounded so cute on the phone.

Alexis was really looking forward to this weekend. But she had to remind her cousin that they could not post pictures. After all, her parents would die early deaths if she did something so stupid after she had been taught not to post personal information on the Internet.

When she arrived home around three that afternoon, Gary called and they talked while she cooked her small pizza and played with her dog, Blackie. Gary promised that he would come to the movie to meet her, and that really excited her. She had to find something to wear so he would not be able to tell that she was only thirteen. She really didn't like lying, but who in the world would believe that she was sixteen? They would have a ball this weekend.

After Alexis finished talking to Gary, she hung up the phone and called Jamestown to get the movie list. She was happy that they would finally be able to meet each other. She had been talking to him for what seemed like forever. He said that he was tall, good-looking and had a nice red T-top Camaro, in which he spent his time flying through the neighborhood, soaking in the sun and the ladies. Alexis was impressed. She had spent many evenings on the phone talking to him, encouraging him to continue their conversations.

Gary was an older boy. He said that he was eighteen years old. In the last couple of weeks he had been really pushing to meet her. He had even suggested that they have sex. But Alexis knew that wasn't happening, so she just ignored the conversation. Plus, she told Demetra, and Demetra said not to worry.

After Alexis contacted the theater and got the information on the movies they would most likely watch, she cleaned her room, then phoned her mother's job.

"Hi, Mom! What are you doing?"

"I'm preparing for my meeting."

"I just called to see what you were up to. You got two messages, but I let them go to voice mail."

"Oh, I'll check the messages a little later. Wash the white clothes for me and clean up your bathroom."

"I already put the clothes in the washer. I'll clean my bathroom up next. Don't forget my Burger King."

"Okay. Remember, no company!"

"I know. You don't have to keep telling me."

"I'll see you later."

"Bye, Momma."

As Alexis put the phone back in its cradle, it rang again. She picked it back up and answered. "Hello."

"Hey, baby."

"Oh! Hi, Gary."

"Can I come by the house?"

"No. I can't have company while my parents are not home."

"Aw, baby. I really want to see you."

"You will tomorrow at the movies."

"Well, don't make a brother beg. I want to see your little fine self today. I can come right over. Let me rock your world."

"What you mean by *rock my world*?"

"You ever had sex, baby girl?"

"Why?"

"I can show your little self some sweet action."

"Well, that's okay." Alexis decided to change the subject. "What do you want to see at the movies?"

"Nothing but you, baby. I want to kiss those pretty, soft lips, and kiss your neck."

Alexis giggled. She had never been kissed before. She was kinda looking forward to it, even though just talking about it made her nervous.

"You so crazy," she said, not knowing what else to say.

"Crazy about you, little lady."

She giggled again. "I'll see you tomorrow."

"Okay. But you gon' give me some of that sweetness."

"Bye." She hung up the phone before he said anything else. It made her a little nervous that he was talking like that. She pushed the numbers on the phone to call Demetra. Letting it ring, she thought about what Gary had said. She was not ready for sex, and he was not even going to convince her about something so serious.

Alexis was jolted out of her thinking.

"Hello," Demetra said.

"Demetra, girl, Gary called talking about he wanted to have sex with me. I am not having sex with him, so you better tell him. I am not playing! I like him, but I am not having sex with no one."

"Girl, slow down and breathe."

"I ain't having sex with Gary."

"I know you are not."

"You better tell him."

"I will. Don't worry, I'll get that fool straight. You just slow your role. Let me handle that brother. I got your back."

CHAPTER 3

Just Hanging Out

Demetra arrived at Alexis' home around six-thirty p.m. Janice picked her up at the Metro Link and brought her to the house. She walked through the house calling out Alexis' name.

"Alexis, girl, where you at?" Demetra walked through the living room and around a short corner to go up the stairs to the second floor. "Girl, where your tail at?"

"Dag, girl, I am up in my room."

Demetra skipped up the steps to see her cousin. As she walked into her bedroom, she hugged her. "So what's up, girl?"

"Nothing. I'm looking for something to wear to the movies."

"I'm just wearing Apple Bottom jeans and my Apple Bottom T-shirt. Why don't you put on one of your Apple Bottom sets?"

"Nah! I think I am going to wear this Rocca Wear set."

"Whatever. What time is the movie?"

"It starts at nine-thirty. But we can leave early and walk around the mall. Is Gary still meeting us?" Alexis asked.

"Heck, no. That boy is too old and stupid for you. You ain't ready to have sex with no one, and he was stupid for suggesting it. Leave his butt alone. Your parents ain't blaming me for messing up your life and getting you pregnant. Plus, you don't know him, anyway. You have never even met him for him to be talking about sex, anyway."

"Well, I guess you are right."

"I know I am. Leave him alone. Don't even talk to him."

"Yeah, alright," Demetra said with very little confidence.

"After the movies I have something to show you on the Internet, anyway."

"Okay. What is it now?"

"Wait and see. Let me get my clothes on so we can go. Your mom is going to let me drive her SUV."

As they got ready to go to the movies, Demetra reminded Alexis to get the speakers for the computer. Then Demetra secured the keys from her aunt and they left. In the car, they played all kinds of music, bopping their heads and shoulders to the heavy sounds of Bow Wow, Tyrese, Ciara and other cool singers. They arrived at the Jamestown Mall and parked close to the theater. As they walked into the electronic doors, they immediately noticed two girls mocking them.

"Look at those ugly chicks staring at us."

Alexis turned to look and smiled. "You so silly."

"Nah! I'm real. I can't stand folks mocking me like that." Demetra turned and rolled her eyes at the girls, who just laughed.

As they walked through the mall, so many guys tried to talk to them, but they ignored them all.

"Girl, look at that guy staring at you." Alexis turned to see this fine guy walking toward them.

She squealed to Demetra, "Girl, he is walking right over to me!" The smile that crossed her lips was humongous. She could not control the way her lips were turning up toward the skylight. They were betraying her. She did not want to seem overly excited, but he was so cute.

"Hey, my name is Cameron." He smiled and showed his perfect, pretty white teeth. He was about 5′6″. He had these cute dreadlocks that hung close to his shoulders, and he had on a pair of Timberland boots and a Sean John blue-jean outfit. He looked to be about fifteen.

"Hi! I'm Alexis."

"That's pretty," he said, as his cheeks blushed red.

"Thanks. Are you here to see a movie?"

"Yeah. My boys and I are going to see 'When a Stranger Calls.'"

"We're going to see that, too."

"Maybe we can sit together."

Cameron introduced his two friends to Alexis and Demetra, and they planned to meet back at the theater before the show so that they could sit together. But first they wanted to go into Macy's to check out the new Baby Phat line.

After the girls checked out Macy's, where Alexis picked out a Baby Phat purse that she would pick up before the weekend was over, they went into the bathroom. There they saw the same two girls they'd seen when they first walked into the mall. The girls were staring at them and laughing. This made Demetra angry.

"What ya'll whores looking at?"

"I know you didn't call me a whore?" the older of the two girls asked. She walked closer to Demetra.

"You don't scare nobody. Jump if you want to, and see what happens." Demetra balled her fist up and started moving around as if she was a boxer. But it took young Alexis to smooth the waters.

"This is stupid. We don't even know you, to be fighting over nothing. Come on, Demetra, let's go. I want to see the movie."

"Nah! They are tripping. Nobody said anything to them in the first place. They have been tripping since we walked into the mall."

Alexis grabbed Demetra's hand and pulled her toward the door. "All's good," she told the girls in the bathroom, and she and Demetra walked out. Neither group of girls wanted to be thrown out the theater, so everybody just decided to chill. Thanks to Alexis' calmness, they'd escaped another one of Demetra's tirades.

Demetra was an angry young lady. She loved Alexis, but in the same breath she also envied her. She felt that Alexis was always the one on the receiving end of gifts, love, admiration and all the things that were positive. She loved her cousin, but still wondered why Alexis had to have the loving parents who paid attention to everything she did. Alexis' parents attended everything that she was involved in, while Demetra's mother was always too sick to do anything.

Demetra wished that her parents cared about her. Her mother never attended anything she was involved in, and she hadn't seen her father in years. Even then, he lied about everything. He was so untrustworthy and never lived up to his promises. If only she'd been the daughter of the Kirby's, life would have been different for her. She would have a late-model car, plenty of designer clothes, and she would not be struggling to get an education. Still, she was just excited to be in the family as a niece, though it would be even better to be their biological child.

She really did love her cousin and would never bring harm to her. Still, Alexis was not perfect. She was sneaky, sometimes conniving, but never overly manipulative. She just tended to hover close to the edge of safety, never quite crossing over or tipping to the bad side. But for once, Demetra wanted to see her get in trouble, even if she had to push her goody butt clean over the edge.

They arrived at the meeting spot at nine-thirty. Cameron and his friends were already there.

"Y'all ready to roll?" Demetra asked, trying to play it cool. She walked away, switching her little butt like she was the finest young thing in the mall. The other boys followed behind her like fire follows gas, but Cameron waited for Alexis.

In the movies, Alexis and Cameron talked whenever they could. Alexis handed him her phone number. At the end of the movies, Cameron kissed her on the cheek and put a piece of paper in her hand. They promised to call each other. Each group headed out separate exit doors.

As Alexis and Demetra walked out the door, a hand suddenly appeared and snatched Demetra's shoulder-length hair. She turned to defend herself, but she found that the hand had closed into a fist and her hair was tightly wrapped around the fist, causing her to twirl and trip over her feet. Alexis had no choice but to jump on the back of the assailant. She grabbed the girl's hair and pummeled her head rapidly with her fist, trying to get her to release Demetra's hair. It was the girl from the bathroom.

The girl's friend suddenly grabbed Alexis, and they all began to fight each other. Demetra put a whipping on the girl who had her in the tight grip. Alexis and Demetra were winning, when suddenly the mall security showed up. All the girls were thrown in the police car and taken to the police station. Alexis started crying. She had never been in trouble and was worried about how her mother would handle the situation.

"Stop crying! You know you acting like a little sissy." Demetra was pissed. Why in the heck was Alexis crying? When things got rough, she always cried for her mommy.

"Shut up, Demetra."

"We beat their butts. So why are you crying?"

Alexis just ignored her and waited on her mother to come to the station.

Once her mother got there and talked to the officers, they let them go with the scared-straight talk. Alexis wasn't worried about ever coming back. Jail was not for her.

As she explained to her mom why she was fighting, Alexis started to cry. "Mom, I was helping Demetra. The girl had her hair wrapped tightly around her hand, and she was disabled. She couldn't do anything, so I jumped on the girl to make her loosen her grip."

"What did I tell you, honey? Fighting doesn't solve anything. It just makes things worse."

"I know, but this time the girl started it and we just finished."

"There are times when you have to walk away. But I understand you want to protect your cousin. This could have been worse. I'm just glad that you both are okay. Next time keep your eyes open, and if you expect trouble, get security."

"I know, Mom. But they snuck up on us!"

"I understand. I just don't want y'all fighting. That's all."

Alexis was so mad that she jumped into Janice's car and pouted all the way to the mall to pick up the SUV. Luckily, they hadn't told the officers that they'd been driving.

In her mind, Demetra was angry at Alexis. She always weaseled her way out of everything.

CHAPTER 4

Breaking the Rules

Later that night, before Janice went to bed, she spent more than an hour talking to the girls. She wanted them to understand that fighting does not solve anything. It just makes things worse. She was beginning to worry that Demetra was a bad influence on her daughter.

Demetra was still pissed at Alexis. "Sometimes you make me sick."

"I don't know what you are so mad about. If I hadn't jumped on that girl, she would have beat you down."

"You are crazy if you think that punk ass girl would have won a fight against me."

"Just leave it alone." Alexis went to her room and changed into her pajamas. She planned to go to bed, since Demetra was still tripping.

When Alexis was lying in her bed, Demetra walked in.

"Are we going to surf the Internet?"

"I don't know. You keep tripping, and I don't have time for your attitude."

"Come on, girl! Let's get on the Internet. You know you are not mad at me, anyway."

Alexis stretched out her legs across the bed and

demanded that her cousin make her get out. "You think you are so tough, make me get up!"

With that, Demetra dove onto the bed and pinned Alexis down. "See, little girl, I could break your neck and you wouldn't even see it coming."

Huffing with anger, Alexis whispered between clenched teeth, "Get off me. Now!"

Demetra jumped up. She saw the fire in her little cousin's eyes. No wonder she had beat that other girl down! Her cousin had some serious anger issues. "Come on, girl. Let's go surf the net."

They went down to the kitchen and grabbed a glass of orange juice. Demetra booted the computer up. They chatted about the fight, laughing at how each other was fighting. It seemed that they had just forgotten about how they made each other so angry. For now, they were on a mission.

"Girl, let's go into a chat room. I found a good one." Demetra opened several windows until she found what she was looking for. "Here it is. Let's post some pictures up."

"I'm not putting my real picture up there. You don't know who would see them."

"You are such a jive turkey. How'd you get so square? My friends said that you were a nerd."

Getting angry again, Alexis pushed Demetra off her computer. "Move! I'll show you who's a nerd." Alexis went to the search bar and typed in Google Image. Once there, she typed in "sexy African-American women." Beautiful women in scantily dressed clothing popped up. She selected one who she felt resembled her. "Here, pick somebody for you."

Demetra selected a mocha-looking woman with shoulder-length hair. She was wearing sexy lingerie. "I like this one."

"Let's post them as our pictures. We can call ourselves Dana and Denise."

"Okay, Alexis. Girl, what has gotten into you?"

"Nothing. They are not us, so they can't be linked back."

"Okay. Where are the new voice speakers?" Demetra was getting excited. This was going to be so much fun, pretending to be someone else.

Alexis jumped up out of her chair, ran to the basement and brought the speakers up. She'd forgotten to get them when Demetra told her to, earlier. "Here they are. I hope they work."

Both girls hooked up the voice speakers with the speed of an expert computer technician. "That was easy!" Alexis snapped her fingers together.

"Girl, we bad," chuckled Demetra.

After the speakers were connected, they started talking to some guy named Steve.

"Hey, what's up, baby girl? Is that your picture?"

Alexis responded, "Yes. Do you have one to post?"

"No, but I will post one later this week. How old are you?"

"Eighteen," Alexis said.

"You look so good in that outfit."

"Where do you live, Steve?" Alexis turned to Demetra and mouthed the words, "This is pretty cool!"

"I live in Atlanta."

Demetra was so anxious that she started firing off questions. "Are you dating anyone? How old are you?"

"Nineteen. Just a year older than you."

"What about my other question?"

"Nah! I'm single."

Demetra fired back, "Yeah, right! Boy, you know darn well you older than nineteen. And you got a woman. And if you don't, what's wrong with you?" Demetra was getting smart with him because she felt that he was lying. So she simply just let him know.

"Ain't nothing wrong with me. I told you, I don't have a girlfriend."

"You know darn well you are older, with that deep-ass voice." Demetra was pissed that he was lying.

"I'm not talking to you, anyway. I'm talking to that sweet thing."

"My name is Dana," Alexis said with a giggle.

"Dana. That's a sweet name."

"Have you been drinking, Mugface? You slurring all over

yourself." Demetra was beginning to get feisty.

"You better get your girl, Dana."

"Denise, stop acting silly."

"How we gon' meet, baby girl? You look so good on that picture. Baby, you got me feeling something for you. You know, I'm definitely into you."

"You so crazy," was all Alexis could say.

"Dana, I don't like him," Demetra said.

Steve was getting angry. "I think you jealous 'cause I am paying more attention to your girl than you." All he could think of was getting with a young honey. If only he could get Dana to get back at him without her jealous girl.

Steve was a thirty-five-year-old pedophile. He had been in jail for six years for molesting a twelve-year-old girl. He liked his girls young, tender and untouched. He spent countless hours on the Internet searching for them, pretending to be younger than he was. Dana sounded young. He had a feeling she was less than fifteen years old, by all that giggling she was doing. He was going to give her his e-mail address and they could continue to talk. He lived in Alabama, but would travel anywhere to meet his prey. That way, no one would be able to track him down.

"Dana, baby, write this down: _Steve12@yahoo.com_. Hit me up when your jealous ass friend not around. You hear me, baby girl? You sound so sweet."

Demetra shot back, "Boy, you are stupid! You will not be hearing from her again."

Janice was tossing around in her bed upstairs. She was

missing her husband and could not sleep. He was away in a business trip. She decided to get up and go get a glass of orange juice. As she walked down the stairs, she heard a man's voice. Rushing into the kitchen, she screamed, "You girls better not have a man in my house!"

"Mom, we are on the Internet," Alexis said quickly.

"I'm not stupid. I hear a man's voice."

"Mom, we are chatting with a friend through Daddy's speakers."

"Get off that Internet now! You are talking to a man."

Alexis disconnected the voice speaker. "Mom, we were talking to a friend."

"Listen, girl, you do not have any men as friends. What did I tell you about that Internet? You can find yourself in a lot of trouble. People lie about themselves. They are not who they claim to be. Do not let me catch you back in those chat rooms! You girls go to bed now!"

"Mom," Alexis whined.

"Mom, nothing! Get your fast butt up those steps. Demetra, I expect more from you. You should be a role model for her, not lead her in the wrong direction."

"Yeah, Auntie, I get blamed for everything. Alexis makes her own decisions."

"Alexis is a very impressionable pre-teen. I expect you to monitor her, not show her how to do things that can get her hurt."

"Auntie, you don't even know your child."

"What do you mean?"

"Nothing, Auntie. Forget I said anything."

"Alexis, I will be discussing this with your father. That man you were talking to was drunk, too."

Alexis stomped upstairs. "Demetra, why you always trying to get me in trouble?"

"Your mother thinks you are so perfect. She doesn't know you like I do."

"Girl, I don't do anything bad. You are not sleeping in my room. Go in the guest room."

Demetra walked into Alexis' room and grabbed her travel bag. "I don't want to sleep in your funky room, anyway. It stinks, and you do, too."

Alexis jumped out of her bed and slammed the door behind Demetra. Demetra was acting weird. *But so what*, she thought. She had Steve's e-mail address and would e-mail him tomorrow.

CHAPTER 5

Stupid Is as Stupid Does

For some reason, the two cousins were not getting along. Demetra was acting like she was jealous of her cousin, and Alexis did not understand why. That Saturday morning, the girls prepared to go to church. The Kirby family was Seventh Day Adventist and attended church on Saturday.

Every week they would load up and drive the thirty-five minutes to East St. Louis to attend church with other relatives. It was a day that the family would get together to worship and spend time together, reminiscing and enjoying each other. They were a very close family. But lately Demetra had been acting different, like she was unhappy or something. Janice decided to get to the bottom of what was going on. She loved her niece and knew that she was a good child, but lately she had been acting out.

As a matter of fact, two weeks ago Janice's sister, Casey, informed her that Demetra had been getting smart with her and she felt that her daughter was out of control. Apparently, they had argued, and Demetra cursed her mom out and ran out of the house. When the mother and daughter talked later, Demetra explained that she was disappointed that her mother never seemed to have time for her. It bothered her.

Demetra said that Casey never supported her, even when she was participating in various school activities. Frustrated that her own mother was never at her track meets or basketball games, she just quit. Why should she be the only one playing a sport whose mother or father never attended? Casey told Janice that although she had apologized, she didn't think Demetra truly accepted it. That's why Janice wanted to help her. She wanted to try to soothe the little lost girl's heart. Maybe it was not too late.

Everyone was getting ready to go to church. The two best friends who were also cousins were still not speaking. They were not really angry at each other, but neither wanted to be the first to start talking to the other again.

Janice broke the silence in the car. "You both know that I was disappointed in you guys last night. What you all were doing is very dangerous. Do you know how many girls, women and even some boys have been molested and murdered dealing with folks on the Internet? It is not safe. Please don't let that happen again. Stay out of those chat rooms. They are places where folks are not who they say they are. Those people are faceless and nameless. They go to the chat rooms to lure unsuspecting people."

"Mom, we were just chatting."

"You don't chat with strangers. Do you know that when you talk to people, many of them have the ability to pretend to be someone other than themselves? They are good actors. You develop a trusting relationship when you spend time talking with people. The difference here is that the people you think you know are not real. They have fake identities. Stay out of dangerous places."

"Okay, Mom."

"Do you hear me, Demetra?"

"Yes, Ma'am."

"You are not too old to get into trouble. Many girls your age have died in situations with people they met online."

"I know, Auntie."

"Just remember what I said."

"We will," the girls said in unison. They both started laughing, which broke the ice and caused them to start talking to each other again.

Demetra and Alexis spent time talking and laughing at church. Demetra passed a note to her cousin that simply said, "Stay out of that chat room. Forget you talked to that dude."

Alexis wrote back, "I'm not stupid. I will."

Demetra didn't know why, but she felt she needed to tell her cousin not to go back to the chat room. Most of the time, Alexis listened to her; and since Demetra had showed her how to get into the chat room, she just wanted to remind her to leave it alone.

Church was very interesting. Pastor Keys said that nowadays people are coldhearted. Also, he said that in the last days people would no longer willingly help one another. A lot of that was happening now.

Alexis and Demetra listened. The pastor spoke in a language that was child-and teen-friendly. His message was for them, too. That's why they didn't mind listening to Pastor Keys. He was a good speaker and he held their interest.

After church, the family ate dinner over at Casey's house. It was a huge family gathering. Everyone was laughing and full of happiness. It was family time. They enjoyed the entire day, and then it was time to leave. Demetra was not going back home with the Kirby's. She had to work the next day.

****

Later that night, Alexis e-mailed Steve. His e-mail address was easy to remember. They chatted back and forth on Yahoo Instant Messenger. Alexis was having fun typing messages to him. He was funny and wrote some silly stuff.

Three months later, Alexis was still instant messaging Steve. Now they were talking on the phone. Alexis and Steve were very friendly with each other. The young and impressionable teen had really started to like the guy she was chatting with. They shared many personal things. Sometimes when Alexis had problems, she would e-mail him and he would respond. They talked on the phone every day when Alexis came home from school. Alexis never told anyone about Steve, not even Demetra.

Steve had started typing messages to Alexis about sex. He wanted to know if she was a virgin. She told him she was. This only excited him more.

One day Alexis received this e-mail from Steve: "Dana, I want to meet you. When are we going to get together?"

She responded, "I don't know."

"You are hurting me, girl. You know how I feel about you. I really like you."

"I like you, too, but we live too far from each other."

Steve had to convince her to either meet him or let him come to her. He was getting tired of trying to gain her confidence. He was ready and wanted to see her soon. "Distance is nothing. I can get to you by car or plane. Just say we can get together this weekend."

"Steve, let's wait awhile."

"Wait on what? You know you turn me on. I need to see you soon, baby. I just want to hold you and touch you."

"Steve, I'm not ready for that."

"Baby, that is why you need me, I can get you ready."

Alexis hesitated to type the next words. "I'm not ready for sex."

"I wasn't, either, but when you fall in love you want to be with the person you love. You love me, Dana?"

"I don't know."

"We have been talking on the phone for almost four months. I know you like me as much as I like you."

Alexis smiled to herself. She was thinking, *He really likes me.* But still, she just said, "You can come here for Labor Day."

"Baby, that is too far away."

"It's only five months away."

"Do you know what we can do with five months to ourselves? Why don' you plan to come stay with me for awhile?"

"That's alright. I'm staying home. But we can meet in September. I'm sure you can wait until then."

Steve was getting frustrated. When I finally meet this girl, I will certainly make her pay for making me beg. She definitely will get a beat down for disobeying me.

CHAPTER 6

Trapped in the House

Alexis came home and fixed herself a sandwich. After she finished eating, the phone rang. It was Demetra.

"What's up, girl?"

"Nothing. Just finished eating a sandwich. Wait, someone is at the door."

Alexis opened the door. "I think this is Gary. I see his red T-top."

"Alexis, don't let him in."

"I already did."

"Give him the phone, now!" As soon as Gary was on the phone, Demetra said, "Boy, if you put your hands on my cousin, you are going to jail forever. Get out of that house."

"Demetra, stop tripping," Gary told her. "I'm just visiting her."

"She is a minor. You touch her and the men in prison will be touching you for a long time."

Gary handed the phone back to Alexis.

"Hello," she said.

"You better not hang this phone up."

Gary tried to kiss Alexis, but she pushed him. "Stop!"

"What is he doing, Alexis?"

"Trying to kiss me."

"Tell him to leave."

"Gary, you have to go now."

"You gon' put me out?"

Just then, the garage opened and a car pulled in. Gary and Alexis were both too afraid to leave. They just stood there. Harrison, Alexis' dad, walked in. When he saw the young man, he grabbed a bat he kept in the corner of the hallway. "What the heck is this man doing in my house?"

"Dad, I told him to leave."

Just then, Gary rushed to the door, opened it and ran out. Harrison was on his heels. The boy jumped into his car and locked the door. Harrison hit the car with the bat as the boy gunned the motor and sped off.

Harrison walked back into the house, too angry to speak. He stood in the living room, gathering his thoughts. He had to breathe or else he would hurt his daughter. He had told her more times than he had fingers and toes not to bring no nappy-headed boy into his home without a parent present. Plus, that knucklehead looked like he was eighteen. Once Harrison calmed down, he was going to beat Alexis' tail, and he didn't care if she was too old or if she called the police. She was too young to even understand the danger she was in.

After Harrison calmed down, he asked his daughter, "Did I not tell you no company?"

"Yes, Dad, but I did not invite him over."

"How did he get in, then?"

"Daddy, he pushed his way in. I told him to leave and he wouldn't. Demetra was on the phone when he did it. She stayed on the phone so he would know that someone knew he was in the house."

"Do you know what danger you were in?"

"Yes."

"You are on punishment. I should beat your butt, but if I do I will hurt you. Get upstairs. I will talk to you when your mother returns home."

Alexis, who had been holding the phone all this time, said goodbye to Demetra. She hung up the phone and took her time going toward the stairs, because she was scared to walk past her dad.

"Go to your room, Alexis. I don't want to see you right now." Harrison was still reeling with anger. As Alexis passed him, he lifted his hand to hit her, but she ran past him and up to her room.

Alexis lay on the bed and cried. She had disappointed her dad. She hated disappointing her parents. They had always been in her corner.

She jumped off the bed, locked her door and booted up her laptop. Once it was ready, she went to her Yahoo account and e-mailed Steve. She told him everything that had happened. Steve said he was very angry and wished he could meet Gary to teach him a thing or two.

"Alexis, I am coming to meet you next Friday. Have one of your friends drive you to the mall that you told me about, at around five p.m. I am coming to protect you."

"I am on punishment forever. My dad will never allow me to go anywhere."

"You are really pissing me off. I am only trying to protect you."

"You don't have to come from Atlanta to protect me here."

"I know I don't. I want to meet you. I want to show you how it feels to be really loved."

"Steve, I can't talk to you anymore. You are acting too weird. I am not ready for sex. Stop asking me."

"Okay, then stop e-mailing and instant messaging me."

Steve signed off before he blew his cool. He was tired of playing this game. He would have stopped e-mailing and talking on the phone with her a long time ago, but Alexis was so young and innocent. He could tell from their many phone calls. Steve decided to call her.

The phone rang. Her dad answered. "Hello?"

"May I speak to Alexis?"

"Who's calling?"

The phone went silent.

"Alexis, come here!"

Alexis came bouncing down the stairs. "Yes, Daddy?"

"Some man just called here asking for you. Who is it?"

"I don't know, Daddy."

"Well, why would he ask for you and then hang up when I

asked who was calling?"

"I don't know."

Her dad decided to check the phone bills and compare the number on their caller ID with any on the phone bill. He couldn't find any copies of their old phone bills. He decided to speak to his wife when she came home.

CHAPTER 7

The Real Deal

When Janice came home from work, her husband informed her about everything that happened. They talked to Alexis. She told them that Demetra had introduced her to Gary, but that she had only spoken to him on the phone. She further explained that he had forced himself into their house. The Kirbys contacted the police. They were ready to file charges, but since nothing had happened and Alexis had been talking to Gary on the phone as a friend, no charges would be filed. Gary never touched or harmed Alexis.

Her parents then contacted the phone company to get new printouts of their calls. What they found out was that Alexis had been destroying the phone bills at Steve's request, so that no one could track his calls. Once they received the printouts, they were horrified to find that their daughter had been chatting with someone from Atlanta for months. But through further conversation with Alexis, they found out that she really had feelings for this stranger. This was so perplexing to her parents that all they could do was ask more questions.

"I don't understand, Alexis. How could you possibly like someone you've never met?"

"We are friends, Momma."

"Sorry, honey. You don't know this person. How do you know if he is who he says he is?"

"I have his pictures."

Her daddy was so frustrated. They could not make this

girl see the dangers of what she was involved in. "Go get the pictures. And we want his entire name."

Alexis got up off the black leather couch in the den and walked upstairs to her room to gather the photos of Steve. She brought them back and handed them to her dad. "Here he is."

"What is his full name?"

"Steve Jacob Johnson," Alexis replied with confidence.

Harrison got up and went to the telephone. He called a friend of his who worked with the police department. He gave his friend the particulars on the story and told him Steve's name, city, and age. His friend said that he would call back in an hour.

Alexis' parents continued to discuss the issue. They were clearly upset and disappointed. They assured her that if she ever did something this risky again, prison would be harder than what they would do to her.

"Alexis, we will put more controls on the computer. You can only use the computer in the kitchen. We will monitor your usage. If we find out that you are visiting chat rooms again, we will limit your computer access to only word processing for your homework." Her dad was livid. He had read so much about predators stalking in chat rooms, hoping to meet young teens. Every day there was something in the paper about this, and he always shared it with his daughter. Harrison could not understand why, after all he had discussed with her, she would still put herself at risk.

"Please tell us, Alexis, why you went against your parents on this issue."

"I don't know. It started as a game with Demetra and me."

"Negative association breeds children who disobey their parents," Harrison said as he tossed the pictures of Steve angrily on the table.

"Don't say that," Janice urged her husband. "Demetra is not a bad influence. All kids do things that disappoint their parents. Alexis knew better. We can't blame this on anyone but Alexis."

The phone rang and Harrison picked it up. "Hello?" He stood there and listened. Finally, he thanked the caller and hung up the phone.

"Alexis, Detective Branson has informed me that they just arrested a Steve Jacob Johnson for the rape and attempted murder of a thirteen-year-old girl in Memphis, Tennessee. And his name is not really Steve. His real name is Donaldson Tisdale. He is a serial sex abuser who spent ten years in jail for the molestation of a ten-year-old girl in Alabama, which is where he really lives. He also spent six years in prison for molesting a twelve-year-old. Not only that, Alexis–he is a thirty-five-old man! He lives in Alabama, but he had a cell phone with a number from Atlanta. I guess that was so he could do his crime and wouldn't be easily tracked."

"Are you sure, Daddy?" Alexis asked through tears.

"Yes. Steve Jacob Johnson was one of his aliases. The FBI was already tracking him, but unfortunately they were a little late. They were able to save the girl before she was murdered, but she was still molested."

"Oh, my God. That poor girl! Alexis, baby, that could have been you. Do you see how dangerous the Internet is when it is misused?" Her mother was crying. As she wiped her tears, she walked over to her crying daughter and asked, "Do you see why we were so adamant about being careful? People are so vicious."

"I understand." Alexis wrapped her arms around both her parents. "I'm so sorry for disobeying you. I won't do it again."

But Janice was still concerned. "What can you do to warn others about this? There is a lesson in this not only for you, but for other kids."

"Since I write for the school newspaper, I can write an article about it."

"Well, you do that. Honey, we love you so much that if anything had happened to you it would have broken our hearts." Her mother lifted Alexis' chin. "Just remember that when you put yourself in harm's way, not only are you hurting yourself, but if something happens to you, you hurt everyone who knows and loves you."

"I'm so sorry!"

"Just don't forget it. The next time you do something like this, the price you pay may be your life."

The Kirbys decided to continue to monitor their daughter and to spend more quality time with her. They also decided that she should participate in more activities to keep her busy. They knew that an idle mind was like the devil's playground, so they enrolled her in several programs at the YWCA, a place where people could go to swim and play sports, learn how to dance and do crafts, and so much more. The programs also picked up the teens from school. Alexis decided to take a swimming and karate class during the first session.

That night, she called Demetra and told her everything. "I told you we shouldn't have been in those chat rooms. He was a rapist and he tried to kill that girl."

"You silly girl, I told you to lose that zero and find a hero. Plus, you didn't even tell me you were talking to him. When your dad called, he was all mad at me, and I didn't even know you were talking to that creep."

"Well, I wouldn't have been talking to him if you hadn't shown me that site."

"Don't blame me!"

"I'm not," Alexis said in a loud voice.

"You know, I thought you were talking to Cameron, anyway." Demetra laughed. "He was cute, too."

"Yeah, but we are just friends. My parents will not let me date, anyway, so I just talk to him on the phone. We met at the movies a couple of times with our groups of friends. But we just cool."

"Girl, remember that Gary?" Demetra asked excitedly.

"Yes. With his stupid self."

"He has AIDS, and he gave it to this fifteen-year-old girl. They arrested him yesterday."

"What!"

"I ain't lying. It was all over the school and stuff. He was going around giving it to people because he was mad that someone gave it to him. His name on the street was Bossman. He made *Jet Magazine*."

"Girl, it ain't safe out here. Folks don' lost their minds. We have to help each other to not make stupid decisions."

"You got that right, cuz."

"Okay, I'll talk to you later. And know that I really do love you."

"Oh, that is so sweet. I love you too, Alexis."

Caught in the Net of Deception

CHAPTER 1

"Don't ever put your hands on me again!"

"I'll touch you when I want to!" screamed Karen. She and her friends surrounded Kelly.

"Stop pushing me!" Kelly was so angry that all she could do was try to get away, maneuvering herself through the crowd of teens.

"You are a loser!" chanted the growing mob.

"Why are you doing this to me? I have never done anything to you!" Tears streamed down Kelly's face as she searched through the crowd, looking for someone with a friendly face–a teacher, a sympathetic student, anyone who understood how it felt to be alone. To be alone, wanting to be popular, attractive and accepted by everyone. Yet as she scanned the crowd, she realized she was indeed alone, without friends or a connection to sanity.

This was her life, trying desperately to fit in, to become visible, to be seen as someone who was loveable, faithful and forgiving. Yet she remained invisible to all the junior high school students. And, although she wanted desperately to fit in and be visible to everyone, right at this second she only wanted to disappear into thin air. Like a poof of powder, she would be gone.

If she was invisible, the pain would go away, because if people could not see her they could no longer hurt her. Kelly was in despair, and so confused. As always, there was no one there to help her escape from Karen and her horrible friends.

****

Kelly Sanders, a brunette, was a nice-looking girl. She was only 5'3" and weighed about 150 pounds. Not your cheerleader type, but she was graceful and kind and she had these absolutely beautiful light green eyes. But even though she often heard from her mother how adorable she was, she never, ever felt it in the presence of her school associates.

She was an A student, thus many of the teens saw her as a nerd and a bookworm. This didn't bother her much, because she knew that education was the key to the future, to her becoming prosperous as well as having the ability to travel and meet new people all over the world. But first she had to come out of this awful shell that caused people like Karen to taunt and tease her.

Kelly was the only child of Mark and Mary Sanders. They were both skilled professionals in the computer industry. Having executive positions in the technical field, they were able to provide their daughter with all kinds of technical toys, including high-speed computers, Internet access, flip video and camera equipment and anything else needed to compete in the high-tech world. Yet even with all this, they found themselves constantly comforting their child and trying desperately to build her self-esteem.

Three years earlier Mark and Mary had had previously sought intervention and help for their daughter. They chose professional counseling after they had found her in the corner of her bedroom, sobbing, on several occasions. She had such a fragile personality, and they knew that if they did not intervene they would lose their only child. Therapy seemed to really help Kelly.

She was diagnosed as suffering from depression. Although she was taking medicine to help control her depression, she still struggled daily with her self esteem issues. It appeared that Kelly was winning the depression battle. At least she wasn't complaining about problems in school.

****

After pushing herself through the crowd, Kelly decided to leave school. It was only eleven o'clock, but her day was already ruined. She went to the book store to browse through the books, and picked up a magazine. All she saw was beautiful, thin teens gracing the pages of the magazine. Not finding anyone who looked like her, she slammed the magazine down and went home. Once there, she retreated to her room, where she cried herself to sleep.

"Kelly, sweetheart, wake up! Wake up, baby girl!" Mary shook her daughter, puzzled as to why she was at home when she should have been in school.

Waking up slowly, Kelly sat up in bed as she gently rubbed the sleep from her eyes. "Hi, Mommy."

"What are you doing home? Are you sick?"

"No, I'm okay." As Kelly swung her legs over to get out of bed, her mother noticed the dark purple bruise on her arm.

"Kelly, what is that on your arm?"

"Nothing. I mean, what?"

"How did you get that big bruise?"

"I don't know."

"What do you mean?"

"Just what I said. It's nothing. I must have bumped into something."

Kelly walked out of her room to avoid further questioning. Mary sat on her daughter's bed, deeply concerned. She wanted to ask, *Are you being bullied at school again?* But she decided to wait until her daughter came to her. "Lord, please take care of my child. Help her to become a happy, well-adjusted person. Please, Lord, help her to find the happiness she deserves. She is such a sweet child," Mary prayed in a low voice. She needed God to hear her.

More than three years ago, Kelly had been the butt of many pranks and high school jokes. She quickly became an outsider. Depressed, she spent countless hours hidden in her room, crying into her pillow. She was so lonely! Her parents did everything to bring her out of the shell, but nothing worked until they sought professional counseling. The one person who was able to reach her was Dr. Danielle Smith. Dr. Smith was a great person, and she and Kelly really clicked. It was because of this that Kelly poured her heart and soul out and was able to get the help she needed to heal her heart. Mary vowed that she would help her child beat her problems and would not allow her to become emotionally violated again without a fight.

That evening at the dinner table, Kelly and her mom and dad chatted about many things. It was not unusual for the family to sit together like this during dinnertime. They were close-knit.

"Kelly, tell Dad what happened today."

"Tell Dad what? Nothing happened."

"What's going on?"

Mom took a deep breath and spoke. "I'm concerned about our daughter. I found her home in bed today. She said that nothing was wrong, but she should have been in school.

Not only that, but she had this bruise on her arm, and she became so upset when I questioned her. I pray that she is not having problems at school again."

"Kelly, you know we love you. Is everything okay, sweetheart?" Dad asked.

"Mom is so melodramatic. I told her that nothing was wrong, but as usual, she won't believe me."

"That's not true! I do believe you. I just want to be sure. This is a family problem, and we have been through it before. I want you to be stress-free and not have problems that you have to deal with by yourself."

"Thanks, Mom, but I am okay. I really did bump into an open locker today, and I had a headache and came home early."

Dad looked at his daughter and wife and spoke slowly. "Kelly, know this: your parents love you, and if you need us we are here for you. Please come to us, because we cannot help you if we do not know what is wrong."

"Thanks, Dad, but everything is just fine. Really mom, it is."

After dinner, while still sitting at the table talking, "Mark and Mary had decided to seek intervention for their daughter, as they did once before, three years ago."

CHAPTER 2

"Hey, skank!"

Kelly continued to walk through the hallway of Clark Johnson High School. She was not going to allow those stupid girls to distract her. Sure, she hated having to weave through the hallways daily, trying to avoid the teasing. But still, today she was going to remain strong.

As she rounded the corner, she suddenly found herself slipping hard on the shining floor. Then she heard loud laughter. Gathering up her books, she turned to see who was laughing and found the source.

"Hey, stupid! I guess we can call you clumsy and stupid now. In addition to being ugly, you have two left feet. Kelly, you sure are screwed up!"

"What's wrong with you, Karen? Why are you so miserable?"

"Miserable! You skanky ass ho, you are the miserable one. Just look at yourself!"

"Yeah, girl, you are a mess," added Samantha. "I don't see how you even get out of bed every day. You are such a bobblehead." Samantha was Karen's best friend and a pain in the ass for Kelly. Everybody just burst out laughing.

"What are you, Samantha? You are nothing but Karen's sidekick. You can't think for yourself."

Samantha lunged at Kelly, snatching her by the hair and popping her hard in the head and face.

"Hit that tramp!" someone in the gathering crowd

screamed.

"Fight! Fight!" others shouted.

Kelly tried desperately to fight back, but she was in a bad position. Samantha had Kelly by the collar and with her free hand she was unmercifully thumping and banging her in the head.

The crowd began to swell. As it did, Kelly was kicked so many times in the side that she almost passed out. All she could do was scream and swing her arms, trying to hit somebody. She quickly grabbed Karen and pulled her down on top of her, but it was the wrong move, because now, with Karen's body on top of her, she could barely move.

Finally, Karen bit down hard on Kelly's jaw. The sound that came out of Kelly's mouth was horrendous. She sounded like a wounded animal. Once Kelly had scrambled up, she kicked Karen hard in her private area. This angered Karen's friends, and before Kelly knew it, so many hands were pummeling her body that all she could do was try to hold them off until help arrived.

As Kelly awoke, she found herself fighting, trying desperately to fend off her attackers. "Stop it, please stop!" She kicked and screamed.

"You're okay, sweetheart. It's me, Mom," said Kelly's mother. She grabbed her daughter's arms and held them stiffly at Kelly's sides. Mom's voice was so soothing that it caught Kelly's attention. This calmed her down.

"Mom, it was so awful! Karen and her friends knocked me to the ground and beat me. I tried hard to fight back, but there were so many of them. I hate them, Mom. I just hate them!" Kelly lifted herself up from the bed and hugged her mother. As Kelly's mother caressed her head and smoothed out her wild hair, she could feel the tears drop from her baby's eyes onto her neck. "I have never done anything to Samantha," Kelly sobbed. "I don't know why they hate me so."

"Who is Samantha?"

"She is Karen's best friend. She is the one who started hitting me."

"Well, I just have to deal with this myself."

"Please, no, Mom! Stay out of it. It will only make things worse. They'll just come after me more."

"I can't stand back and let them do this to you. No child should go through something like this alone."

"You don't understand, Mom. If you get involved, they'll think I am a momma's baby and will harass me more. Please, Mom, stay out of it! Please!"

"Sweetheart, I love you more than anything, and I will not allow my child to be beaten and put into the hospital while I just stand back and let it happen."

Pulling out of her mother's loving embrace, Kelly lay back on the hospital bed and closed her eyes. She was tired and did not want to talk anymore. She knew that her mother dearly loved her, no matter what, but she feared what her involvement would do. Would it cause the girls to harass her even more? Would people call her more names, like fatso, ugly, and now, momma's girl? She didn't want to think about it. She just waited until her mother left, and then she turned over and cried herself to sleep.

CHAPTER 3

The following day, Mary contacted Dr. Danielle Smith. Dr. Smith had worked with Kelly previously, after she attempted to commit suicide. More than anything, Kelly's mom needed the guidance of the psychiatrist again.

"Hello, Dr. Smith. This is Mary Sanders."

"Hi, Ms. Sanders. How are you?"

"Well, I am fine, but I am calling you about Kelly. It seems that Kelly is going through a lot with the kids at her school. They've been teasing and harassing her. She is in the hospital."

"Did she try to commit suicide?"

"No, but I am afraid that she will."

"What happened?"

"Kelly was jumped at school by the same girls who have been bullying her over the last three years. I just wish that I could do something about it."

"Ms. Sanders, you need to transfer her to another school. Take her away from the problem."

"This would be the third time she would be transferred. The problems keep returning."

"We'll have to help Kelly build her self-esteem. As I told you before, bullies choose their prey based on their potential victims' level of self-esteem. They can smell fear and uncertainty."

"It's difficult to feel positive when you are the butt of your classmates' jokes."

"I understand. What hospital is she in?"

"She is in Children's Hospital."

"Okay. I will go see her first thing in the morning."

"Thanks, Dr. Smith. I appreciate any help you can give. I am so tired of this."

"As a matter of fact, I am going to suggest that you see someone, also. You see, this is a family problem, and both you and your husband will need counseling, too. Watching your only child go through so much is quite painful. You will both need to understand what she is going through and learn how to help her through it. I will give you a referral to a really nice doctor who specializes in family counseling."

"Thanks again, Dr. Smith. I guess I may see you at the hospital tomorrow."

"If for any reason we miss each other, I will contact you to schedule an appointment. I want you to know that we will do what we can to make Kelly strong. As a team, we will put all our efforts together. But as you know, Kelly will have to give one hundred percent, too."

"She will, because we will work hard with her."

As Mary hung up the phone, her mind wandered back to the time when Kelly was ten and went through the bullying and teasing about her weight, her looks, and just all the things that kids tease each other about. Kelly did not handle the teasing well, and she tried to take an overdose of sleeping pills, but Ms. Sanders found her before any damage could be done. Finding her daughter unconscious was the worst thing a parent could experience. That day, Mary herself could have died. Now, with every ounce of strength in her body, she promised herself that this time was going to be different. No one would hurt her daughter again without serious consequences.

****

Kelly lay in bed, weeping. This time, she refused to stay at school and be taunted. She was going to transfer and start over, since she didn't have any friends, anyway. But before she left, she had a score to settle.

First, she needed to call Samantha. As Kelly grabbed the phone, she tried to think of what she would say. Finally, after thinking for a few minutes, she slowly dialed Samantha's number. To her surprise, a young girl answered the phone. Kelly didn't know Samantha had a sister.

"May I speak to Samantha?"

"This is she. Who am I speaking to?"

Kelly was shocked that Samantha sounded so young on the phone. She didn't recognize her voice, and this threw her for a loop.

"I said, who am I speaking to?"

"It's Kelly Sanders."

"Why are you calling me, fat whore?"

"What did I ever do to you?"

"You exist!"

"I hope that you get what is due you. You are nothing

but a flunky. Do you ever think for yourself? Are you just following Karen around, smelling her ass?"

"You are so stupid! I am not a flunky."

"Pray that Karen never turns on you."

"That will never happen, because I am not weak like you. You are so weak and desperate."

"Okay. If that is how you feel ..."

"Rot in hell, slut. Fat trick!" With that, Samantha slammed the phone down hard into its cradle.

Kelly hung the phone up. She lay back on the bed and just shook her head. "Lord," she said as she looked at the ceiling, "please help me!"

****

"Hello, Karen."

"What's up, Sam?"

"You will never believe who called here."

"Who, girl?"

"That skank, Kelly."

"What did her stupid fat—"

"Girl, stop! You are so crazy." Sam was laughing so hard she dropped the phone.

"Girl, you need to stop tripping!"

"I know. But guess what she said."

"What?"

"She said I better hope that you never turn on me."

"No, she didn't! Okay, I am going to get her. I got a plan. Ms. Kelly got me suspended and in trouble with my parents, and I owe her a major payback. She will pay for being a lying heifer and getting me into trouble."

"I'm in, too, because she got me put out. I owe her dearly. I mean, what's to lose? We both got suspended, and this is definitely going to affect my grades. We can't go back this semester."

"I know. And I just got my home school teacher, so I am still going to be behind in all my classes.

"Me, too. So we owe her, for sure."

"I'll hit you back later to tell you my plan."

CHAPTER 4

Kelly and Dr. Smith were sitting in the hospital room, talking. The doctor wanted Kelly to explain to her how she was feeling. "Kelly, before the incidents, how were you feeling about yourself?"

"I'm not sure."

"Let me ask you another way. After our last treatment plan, you began to have noticeable improvements. You stated that you felt more empowered, as if you could accomplish anything. Also, you felt powerful enough to handle people's negative impressions of you. For a while, your mom said that you were strong."

"I was, Dr. Smith. For a long time no one could upset me or make me feel bad about myself."

"What changed?"

"Too much pressure, I guess. After people tease you so much, you just give up."

"How long has this been going on?"

"Not too long, maybe a month. I tried to handle it, but it got out of hand."

"Have you been taking the medicine that was prescribed?"

"No, I haven't taken it in awhile."

"Do you know the last time you took your medicine?"

"About five months ago."

"First, let me explain this to you as I did before. You

should never stop taking medication unless the doctor tells you to do so. Stopping medications can trigger other problems. I am not saying that this is what caused your problems at school, but it could have caused you to react a certain way."

"I thought that since I felt better, it was okay to stop taking the meds."

"As I said, when you stop taking medications suddenly, it can cause a host of other physical problems. Going cold turkey could trigger serious panic attacks, anxiety attacks, suicidal tendencies, depression, strong tremors, sudden weight problems (either gaining or losing weight) and many more problems, depending on what medications you are taking."

"Wow! I didn't realize how serious this was. I am so sorry. I could have really hurt myself."

"Well, now that you know, we'll put you back on your medication and then monitor you accordingly. But I do want you to return to your sessions. I have talked to your primary physician, and we are working together to address this problem and to monitor your medication."

"Okay."

"I'll talk to your mom and set up weekly sessions again. Do you have any questions about anything?"

"Do you think that people will ever stop bullying me?"

"Yes, I do. As you move forward, don't ever hesitate to seek the support of your mom and dad, myself, and your teachers and school administers. We are here to assist you as you grow throughout this therapeutic process.

Eventually, you will discover your own coping skills for handling uncomfortable situations. Initially, you may have to change schools to get a fresh start."

"I understand."

"It was nice seeing you today, but not under these circumstances. I will continue working with your parents and the school counselor."

"Thank you."

"I look forward to seeing you in my office next week."

****

Two days later, Kelly was released from the hospital. As a gift to make her feel better, her parents bought her a new laptop computer. Kelly stayed on the computer all week. She was being home schooled at the moment and would return to a new school next month, but for now she completed her homework and surfed the net. She entered chat rooms and met a lot of new friends.

On Saturday, Kelly heard the phone ringing. She jumped up out of bed and ran to the kitchen to answer it.

"Hello."

"Is this that big funky ass pig?"

"Who is this?"

Kelly heard the click of the phone hitting the cradle. She laid her head on the table and cried silently. *Will this ever stop? Will my heart ever stop breaking?* She was so hurt, she didn't think she could take more pain. Why couldn't she be the lucky one whose personality was so vibrant that to be friends with her, you would have to wear shades?

As she sat there crying, her mom walked into the kitchen. "Kelly, what's wrong, sweetheart?"

Before Kelly could open her mouth to respond, the phone rang again. Mary grabbed it angrily. "Hello!"

"Where is your fat ass daughter?"

"I don't have a fat ass daughter. Please don't call here again.

Embarrassed, Mary hung the phone up. "Kelly, I am so sorry that I let that caller take me there. I am so tired, too, of you being hurt. You don't deserve that kind of treatment from anyone. Please, sweetheart, don't let these spineless kids change your loving heart. You don't have to go back to that school. Your dad and I found another school for you to attend. Tomorrow we can go check it out, if you are up to it."

"Thank you, Momma." Kelly laid her head on her mother's shoulder. "Why don't people like me?" she wanted to know.

"It's not that people don't like you. People are fickle and they follow the wrong crowd. Most people look for acceptance any way they can get it, and a lot of these teens are followers and not leaders."

"You would think that people would think for themselves."

"They don't. People are weak. Being in the in crowd is what they seek. Oftentimes, they participate in hurting others because they are happy they're not the ones who are being teased. So to keep the focus off themselves, they join the crowd."

"That's so stupid."

"Well, aren't teens stupid around this age? I'm not agreeing with this kind of behavior, but I do want you to understand human behavior. Teens do stupid stuff. Some of them actually regret it later, but there are some who are just ornery and mean. Those are the ones we have to be careful around."

"Ooooh! I just want it to all stop."

"It will, baby. It will. Now, let's get you something to eat."

CHAPTER 5

Karen Patrick stood 5'8" in her stocking feet. Most people thought she was a model because of her fresh, sparkling skin, which smelled of fresh-picked strawberries. She was a shapely girl who spent many hours working out with her friends on the cheering squad.

Karen had grown up in a home where it was not uncommon to find her family members in separate rooms, doing their own thing. Her parents, Jim and Teresa, were both successful professionals, project engineers for competing companies. But although they were loving toward Karen, they were never touchy-feely with each other. They spent a lot of time screaming at each other or working alone in their offices on their computers, and they never showed each other any loving emotions.

Although they were financially well off, they stayed close to their home. Their neighbors did not know them well, but most of the kids in the school did, because their only daughter was a popular cheerleader. Many of the teens spent countless hours in their home.

Jim and Teresa still acted like teenagers themselves, never disciplining their daughter because in their eyes she could do no wrong. Rarely did they spend time with their child. When Teresa had the time to talk to Karen, they would surf the net together, pretending to be folks they were not. It was a lot of fun just going into the different chat rooms, teasing the boys and taunting unsuspecting teenage girls. They had so much fun being mean to others. Pretending to be someone they were not was nothing but fun; they honestly thought that no one would get hurt.

As they sat playing on the computer, Karen told her mother that she was ready to return to school. "I've been sitting out of school for two weeks because of that fat blimp. She is so weak, and always crying to the teachers. She got me and Samantha kicked out for the rest of the year. I am definitely going to pay her back."

"Yeah. She is costing us money, since you are going to have to go to a private school. We are taking on the financial burden of your being kicked out of school. That whining heifer is causing us too many problems."

"Mom, I am going to get her back."

"How? I don't think you should do anything. I don't want you to get into more trouble."

"Nothing is going to happen. I am going to create a MySpace page and pretend to be somebody else"

"What is a MySpace page?"

"Mom, you are so old! It is a popular net work that people use to socialize. You can get involved with a network of friends; write a personal profiles, and blogs. Remember when I showed you the site that I blog on? Well, MySpace is different because it allows you to network with friends by inviting them to your page. You can send messages, remember birthdays and invite people to activities or events."

"Oh, yeah. I recall you telling me about this. So what do you plan to do?"

"Since Kelly is such a loser, I plan to act like I am interested in becoming her friend. This is a way for me to keep up with her. If she is saying negative stuff about me, I can send it off to our huge network of classmates."

"So how are you gonna get her to talk about you?"

"I haven't thought that far yet."

"Does she have a boyfriend?"

"Get real! Who wants to date her? She is fat."

"Don't get it twisted."

"You trying to be cool, Mom?"

"Nah! I'm just saying, boys do like fat girls, no matter what they say. They may not want people to know, but have you noticed that many fat ladies are married?"

"Yeah, but they got that way after marriage, I bet."

"Honey, you are so young. Men marry fat girls all the time–maybe more than they marry thin ones."

"Yeah, right!"

"I'll tell you what. Why don't you pretend to be a boy named Nicholas and act like you are interested in dating her? Send her some poems and stuff like that. I bet she'll fall for that."

"Wow! That sounds like a good idea."

Karen went to turn on the computer. While she waited on the computer to boot up, she called Samantha. She waited while the phone rang. Finally, Samantha answered the phone.

"Come over! Mom helped me to come up with a good idea to keep up with what Kelly is saying about us."

"Oh, girl, I am on my way over."

Once Samantha arrived, she, Karen and Karen's mom surrounded the computer terminal. It was now time for Karen to tell her mother and Samantha the details of her plan. The moment was intense, yet exciting. Teresa wanted her daughter to be happy, and she didn't necessarily care how she achieved that happiness, so being part of a triangle with her friends was nothing new.

"Explain to me what you are going to do," Samantha requested as she pulled her chair closer to the computer screen.

"First, I am going to locate her profile. Mom, see, all you have to do is go to the MySpace home page. I already set up the fake boy's e-mail account. Now we'll become a member of MySpace, using the name Nicholas Smith. Now we have created a fake person. Next, just go to the search bar and enter the person's name we want to invite to be Nicholas' friend. We'll ask about thirty people, so Kelly will think this person has some friends. To find the person you want to invite, you can also enter the state they are from. See, I entered Kelly Sanders. See all the Kelly's that come up?" Karen scrolled down the names. "There she is. Her picture is posted. Then, I'll click here to ask her to become a friend. She'll e-mail this boy, who will claim to be interested in her. But she is really e-mailing me."

"This is such an awesome idea!" Samantha and Karen high-fived each other, slapping their palms against each others' open hands to show that they were proud of what they were doing.

Karen worked hard to create her new MySpace page. She was a graphic artist and had an excellent eye for creating things. Her mother eventually left to cook dinner, but Karen often called her and informed her about what she was putting on the page. Teresa would give her advice to make things sound good, as Karen/Nicholas wrote a blog about what kind of girl he was interested in.

Karen finished the first comment and posted it. Hi! Thanks for visiting. My name is Nicholas and I am a member of a basketball team. We are so good that we are participating in our state's final competition. I am so excited! What would make it even better is if you visit my profile often and get to know me. Maybe next year you can attend one of our games.

Next, Karen added fake pictures from Google Image of a very handsome boy of about seventeen years of age.

"Mom and Samantha, everything is set. Let's see if she responds."

Karen and Samantha continued to surf the net while Teresa finished cooking.

CHAPTER 6

Kelly was bored. Since she had been released from the hospital, she was feeling lonely. As she read her book, *The Skin I'm In,* by Sharon Flake, she started to feel a lot better, knowing that others were going through the same thing. When she grew tired of reading, she decided to check her MySpace page. Since her release from the hospital a week earlier, that was all she found herself doing.

As Kelly logged into her account, she noticed that she had fifteen requests for new friends. She clicked on each request and visited their sites. She wanted to know who was asking to become friends before she actually accepted. When she finally visited Nicholas Smith's site, she was impressed. He was cute, and his profile stated he was single and straight. She decided to accept his invite and also to send a message to his inbox. She wrote, *Hi, my name is Karen. Thank you for inviting me to be a friend. Nice picture. Stop and visit as much as you like.*

She really didn't think much about the message, because it never occurred to her that she would receive a response. But two days later, when she logged on, she found this message: *Hi, Kelly. Thanks for accepting my request. Tell me more about you. I like your picture.*

Kelly smiled and tried to think of something cute to say in response. Hi, Nicholas. I like reading poetry. I like talking and I am very creative. I enjoy drawing and I love basketball. Thanks about the picture.

****

On the other side of town, Karen, Teresa and Samantha were cracking up. Kelly grabbed her side because she was laughing so hard. "This was too easy. She bit the bone quick."

"That's because she is so desperate," Samantha chimed in. "Let me post the next message."

"Mom, you write a poem. You can be Nicholas, since so many boys like fat girls. I'm sure you'll know exactly what to say to fat Karen."

They all laughed as Samantha crafted her new message and Teresa wrote the poem.

"Okay. Here is the message I wrote," Teresa said.

Hi, Kelly. You are a dime for real. I am so glad that you are not retched. You are so cute I wrote this poem for you. You are a friendly face, visiting me on MySpace. I'd like to be friends, and spend time together that never ends.

"Mom, that poem is so lame!" Karen read it again and laughed.

"Mark my words, she is going to like it."

Samantha hit send. "Now let's wait to see what Ms. Deadbeat is going to say when she sees this."

They all laughed. Teresa was having fun hanging with the teens. Jim was never at home, so having someone to chat with eased her loneliness. Plus, she enjoyed spending time with her only child. She was happy that she was seen as one of those parents other teens wished they had. Karen told her that the cheerleaders and others said they loved her mom because she was so cool. Teresa saw nothing wrong with the games they were playing, and she was glad her daughter was so popular.

"Mom, Samantha and I are going to the mall. Can I use your car? Kelly probably won't respond until tomorrow."

Teresa tossed her keys to Karen. "Drive safely, okay?"

"No problem, Mom. I'll be careful. See you later."

****

After Kelly finished reading *The Skin I'm In*, she tossed the book on the bed. Thinking about Nicholas, she jumped off the bed and headed over to her computer. She logged onto her account and immediately saw the inbox message.

Hi, Kelly. You are a dime for real. I am so glad that you are not retched. You are so cute I wrote this poem for you. You are a friendly face, visiting me on MySpace. I'd like to be friends, and spend time together that never ends.

She smiled and reread the message. This was so neat, to have a guy write her! She had never received any notes or attention from a guy before, so she was too excited. She sent another message.

Hi, Nicholas. What a nice poem you wrote! I really enjoyed it. You are really good with words. I was so impressed. I thought I would give it a try.

I like the poem you wrote for me, so sweet and such a good treat, I can't wait until one day we meet.

She smiled. Not the poetry type, but she enjoyed playing with words. She was kinda impressed with her response. She hit the s button.

****

At the Galleria mall, the girls visited The Cheesecake

Factory after shopping at several of the stores. As they ate their cheesecake, they laughed about how easy it was to fool Kelly.

"I can't believe how easy it is to do this! I mean, anybody can set up a fake MySpace page and check out their competition or see what people are saying about them, or just check out what they are doing, period."

"Karen, you are so right! I would have never believed it would be this easy to play on Kelly. She is so naïve and weak."

"I see why she is so easy to manipulate. She just doesn't get it."

"Damn! She is so useless!"

"I know," Karen said as she stood to throw away her trash. "Let's go back and see if she's responded. She is probably at home, sitting and waiting on Nicholas to respond."

They laughed. Samantha linked her arm through her best friend's, and they walked out the door to the parking lot to find the car.

Once they returned to Karen's house, they went straight to the computer. As they logged on, they heard the front door chime. Teresa entered the house.

"Karen, where are you?"

"In my room, Mom."

They heard Teresa running upstairs. "I was across the street, talking to Marissa. I saw y'all pull into the driveway."

"Mom, we are about to see if Kelly responded." Karen

scanned the computer screen. "Oh, sucky-sucky! She responded already. I knew her desperate butt would."

"Karen, you are so silly."

"No, I am accurate. Remember that!"

"What did she send?" Teresa bent down and glanced over her daughter's shoulder. "I want to know what she said."

"Mom, you need some friends," replied Karen. Everybody giggled. Karen read the message aloud.

Hi, Nicholas. What a nice poem you wrote! I really enjoyed it. You are really good with the words. I'm so impressed. I thought I would give it a try.

I like the poem you wrote for me, so sweet and such a good treat, I can't wait until one day we meet.

"Oh, my God! What a lame poem." Samantha was laughing so hard.

"Yes, this girl is so lame and fat. Look at what she said. *You so sweet and such a good treat.* She can't stop thinking about food, with her fat ass."

"Karen, that's enough. No cursing."

"Sorry, Mom. It slipped."

Samantha stopped laughing long enough to say, "Let's write back now."

Teresa sat in the seat next to Samantha. "Move over so I can respond again. I'll write another poem." She hit reply and typed for a minute. Then she read the new poem aloud.

Hi, Kelly. I like that poem. You are so smart. I also think you are pretty. I wrote this poem especially for you: Computer friends I hope we are. You are so pretty, you could be a shining star. I'm glad that we met, and hope to meet you soon. I think you are so cute; you make me feel like I'm floating to the moon.

Karen groaned. "Mom, you are going to have to come up with something better than that!"

"Trust me, sweetheart. This will seal the deal."

"Okay, Mom." Karen hit send.

"I'll check you girls out later." Teresa left the room.

After visiting several other MySpace pages, Samantha went home and Karen prepared for bed.

Karen showered and went to sleep. The last thing she heard was her mother and dad talking. She thought about how much she missed school, her cheerleading and all her friends. This made her even angrier with Kelly. She thought, *Kelly, you are going to pay for getting me expelled!*

CHAPTER 7

Kelly had an appointment with Dr. Danielle Smith. She got ready and put on her prettiest blouse that matched her new jeans. She was smiling because she had a new friend. Even though she had never met Nicholas, she felt they would be friends for a long time. After all, he sought her out because he thought she was pretty. This made her feel special.

For so long she had been down on herself, because she felt like no one other than her mother and dad cared about her. She was happy to have them, but everybody needed a friend. She was looking forward to reading her next message. That is why she dressed in the sunny, pretty blouse. She felt vibrant. If there was such a thing as feeling good as the sun, she would be bursting with good feelings in her yellow-and-green blouse.

As she walked to the car with her mom, Kelly hummed a little tune.

"Someone is happy. You look so cute today. Why are you smiling?"

"Dag, Mom, I can't smile if I want to?"

"It's not that. In the last weeks or so, you have been so sad. So, sweetheart, it is so good to see your beautiful smile." Mary grabbed her daughter and hugged her.

"Stop, Mom, before someone sees you." Kelly loved the affection her mom showed her, but as with any teen, she didn't want her mother to know it. Pulling away, she opened the car door and jumped into the passenger seat. They drove to the doctor's office discussing various topics. Mary was happy to have her child back.

They walked into the reception area of the doctor's office, and Mary signed in so that the nurse would know they had arrived. Then they took seats and waited until the nurse came out to call Kelly's name. As they waited, Mary asked her daughter again to share what had changed to make her so giddy.

"Mom, I'm just happy, that's all. Nothing special happened. I'm just feeling a little better. Maybe the medication is working."

Mary decided not to continue badgering her daughter. She would just accept the fact that her child was getting better with the medication and the intervention from the doctor. As Mary reached into her purse to pull out her Sony E-book Reader, the nurse opened the door and called Kelly's name.

They both stood up and walked into the doctor's office. As they walked to the full-sized, plushy burgundy chairs, Mary extended her hand to shake the hand of Dr. Smith.

"Hi, Dr. Smith. It's good to see you today."

"How are you?"

"I'm fine, and Kelly has been doing quite well."

"Is that so, Kelly? You look so beautiful in that absolutely gorgeous blouse."

"Everything is fine, thank you."

"Tell me, Kelly, have you been keeping a journal like we discussed last time we met? If so, has documenting your feelings helped you?"

"I really enjoy writing in my journal. I feel safe there. I can document my feelings about so many things. I also get a chance to go back and review how I was feeling on a certain day. I can see what was going on to make me feel bad."

"Journaling is a good way to look back on feelings and attitudes. When you write in a journal, it enables you to learn more about yourself and why you do the things you do."

"I have noticed that Kelly spends a lot of time writing in her journal," Mary said. "I also noticed that when she writes in the journal, it seems to lift her feelings."

"This is because journaling is a way to unlock your inner creativity and promote self-healing. It also helps the writer to gain confidence and to take control of issues that are bothering her."

"I feel good when I write. I dunno, it seems to free me somehow."

"That's great, Kelly. You have discovered the many benefits to journaling. Tell me how often you are writing."

"Every day. Some days I write in it twice. It just depends on what I need to say."

"I'm glad that journaling is helping you. What about the medication? How do you feel about taking the pills?"

"At first I felt somewhat nauseated and dizzy, but that stopped."

"How are you feeling now?"

"I feel much better."

"Please let your mother know if you experience any vomiting or headaches. If that occurs, we will change your medication."

"Okay."

"Mary, I want you to pay close attention to Kelly for the next couple of weeks. When people start taking this type of medication, there may be side effects. You must take notice and watch for any changes in her behavior, including an increase in agitation, crying, and thoughts about things that are not healthy."

"I understand the side effects. I read all the literature that came with the medication, so I am definitely paying close attention to any changes I see. I also asked Kelly to share her feelings about anything. I let her know that I would not be judgmental."

"Great! If you don't mind, I would like to spend the rest of the time talking to Kelly. You can wait in the reception area. We shouldn't be too long."

After Mary left the room, Kelly and Dr. Smith talked about Karen and Samantha. Kelly also said that she was writing poetry and would share some of it with Dr. Smith at her next visit. Kelly never told the doctor about her new friend on the Internet.

Dr. Smith was pleased with Kelly's progress. They scheduled another appointment for the following month.

****

Kelly and her mom had lunch and went to purchase new clothes at the Galleria. Kelly bought new Baby Phat sandals, an Apple Bottom pair of blue Capri jeans and a matching shirt. She was feeling extremely happy until she walked into the bathroom. As she entered the stall to relieve herself, she thought she heard familiar voices. Thinking she was hearing things, she shrugged it off. But when she opened the door and walked toward the sink, she felt someone push her.

"I know this ain't that ugly bitch who got me expelled."

"Come on, Karen," Samantha pleaded. "She is not worth us getting into trouble again."

Karen ignored the pleas of her friend and pushed Kelly violently into the wall. "You skank whore, you think you are all that, but you ain't nothing but a stupid, no 'count pig! You are so fat and ugly that you should just curl up and die." She slammed Kelly into the wall again.

Kelly tried to fight back. She flung her arms out, but Karen's anger and hatred seemed to give her extra strength. Kelly squirmed under the strength of her nemesis. Finally, she gathered enough strength to fight. Swinging her fists, she connected with Kelly's face. Being hit hard in the face made Karen suddenly lose her edge, which almost gave Kelly an opportunity to escape–until Samantha stuck her foot out, causing Kelly to fall on the ground. Violently, the two girls stomped her while she screamed and covered her face and head. She was screaming so loud that someone opened the door and hollered for security. This made Kelly's mom look up from shopping and run toward the restroom, but the security team would not let her in.

One security guard pulled the girls off Kelly and another picked her up off the floor. Kelly's nose was bleeding and she had scratches all over her face and arm.

"They jumped me!"

"Come with us to the office. We are going to call the police department. They will settle this."

As the security guards walked with the three girls, Mary rushed at them and grabbed her daughter. "You will pay for this!" she warned Karen and Samantha. "We are pressing charges."

After the police came and interviewed the girls, they arrested Karen and Samantha.

"You ain't nothing!" Karen said to Kelly as they walked out of the mall to get into the police car.

Kelly and her mom drove to the police station and pressed charges. Then Mary contacted her lawyer so that she could start the procedures to file a civil lawsuit.

"Kelly, sweetheart, they will not get away with it this time. I think they have bought themselves a huge problem. They will pay this time."

"I'm so tired of them, Mom. I just don't understand. I can't go anywhere without having to fight my way out. Why don't they just leave me alone?"

"They will not leave you alone because they are ghetto and come from families that do not make them stand up like respectful, positive young ladies. They are very negative and unhappy people. These girls need God and home training, and they need to listen in class, because they come across as uneducated fools."

"I just want this to stop!"

"Trust me, it will. And sooner than you think."

Mary held her daughter as Kelly silently cried on her mother's shoulder. All Mary could think about was payback. But she knew she would have to use her brain and not her fists.

When they arrived home, John was there. Mary explained everything. John was more than angry. He was pissed off. "They will not get away with hurting my child!" He rushed to his daughter and hugged her. "This will not happen again, I promise you." He left the house.

When he returned, he told his wife that he had gone to Karen's home and spoken to her mother. "I can't believe that woman! She was so stupid. She said that we should let the girls work this out. How could she be so stupid, when she knows that all her daughter and her friend do is jump Kelly?"

"Now you see that the apple does not fall too far from the tree. Karen's mother probably acted or acts the same way."

"Well, let me assure you of this: this time they will not get away with assaulting my daughter." John walked into his home office and slammed the door.

Kelly had long ago retreated to her bedroom. She turned on her computer and went to her MySpace page. Then she went to her inbox to read her messages.

CHAPTER 8

Kelly saw that Nicholas had sent her a response. She smiled. She leaned forward, as if this made the message even better to read.

I want to meet you. You are absolutely a nice, beautiful person. Let's meet at the Starbucks on North Lindbergh on Friday, at six p.m. I can't wait to meet you.

Kelly was so excited. She couldn't wait. It would take all the strength she could muster to make it through the week until she could finally meet him. She couldn't wait to see him.

She went to bed, feeling a little better. As she lay there, waiting on sleep, she thought about what she would wear and wondered what Nicholas would think of her. She had never had a boyfriend or known of any boys who were even interested in her. Most of the guys ignored her or simply called her fatso. The sad part was that she wasn't even fat. Kelly was bigger than the average cheerleader, but she was of average size. She was in the ninth grade, and most of the ninth-graders wore about a size five or seven. She wore a size thirteen, but it didn't look bad. Heck, they all shopped from the junior department, so what was the big deal?

Kelly was so tired! She wanted to have a good life and be happy like everyone else. How could she do that? How could she keep worrying about who liked her and who was against her? Maybe now that she had a friend in Nicholas, everything would be fine. She pulled the covers over her head. Finally, sleep came.

****

The next morning, Mary talked to her lawyer about their civil suit. She felt that the lawsuit would let the other family know that her family would not tolerate any more problems from the girls or their families. After making the call, Mary felt revived. She went into the kitchen and cooked her family a big breakfast. She cooked cheese grits, turkey bacon, turkey ham, soft scrambled eggs and waffles. She felt good and wanted her family to have a great start today.

As the family awoke, showered and came to the kitchen for breakfast, Kelly thanked her parents for their love and support. "Mom and Dad, I am the most blessed girl in the world to have such supportive parents. When my world feels dark, you lighten it. Please know that I will always love you. You mean the world to me, and you have raised a daughter who loves hard, cries often, but who will never hurt others and disrespect adults. Don't ever doubt my love for you."

Mary wiped the tears that ran down her face. "Darling, you are a joy to be with. You have made us happy and proud to be the parents of such a lovely child. We love you dearly. Don't ever doubt our love."

"I don't doubt it, Mom."

John was beside himself with emotion. He didn't want his family to see him crying, but Kelly needed to know that men cried, too. "Kelly, you are the light that guides my heart when it hurts. You are the joy when I smile. Never have I wanted to take care of anyone like I care for you and your mother. You make me so happy! I enjoy being your dad."

"I'm so sorry to give you problems."

John got out of his seat and went over to hug his child. "You are never a problem to us. Always know that! No one could love a child as much as we love you. You are not a problem."

As he kissed his daughter on the jaw, her eyes shone and the smile on her face emitted nothing but the joy of her heart. "Thank you, Mom and Dad."

"You don't have to thank us. We love you. Thank you for being so kind and gracious. You are the love of our life."

After breakfast, the family went into the living room and decided to watch television for awhile. They planned to go visit relatives the next day after church. Kelly said she wanted to see her cousins.

They spent the day as a family. They played board games and simply enjoyed being together. In the afternoon, they went to the park for a walk.

Later that day, Kelly and Nicholas sent instant messages to each other. Every now and then, Kelly would stare at Nicholas' picture. She could not wait until she met him. After they were done with the instant messages, they said goodnight. Then Kelly laid out her clothes for church.

Sleep came easily. Kelly was so happy. The scratches on her face had healed, and with a little makeup her face would be flawless when she met her new friend.

****

Saturday was a beautiful, sunny day. The family prepared for church and went on their merry way. Kelly talked to some of her church friends. One girl asked if they could do something together the following weekend. They planned to go roller skating next Saturday. The girls visited for a while and even sat together through the church service. Kelly was so happy. She felt that she was finally going to have a boyfriend.

The rest of the day was spent visiting relatives. Kelly's grandmother had prepared a great dinner for the family. They feasted on turkey, chicken, greens, Kraft Macaroni and Cheese and broccoli rice casserole. Everything tasted great.

While she was helping Gram with the dishes, Kelly told her that she loved her. "Gram, you know I love you, right?"

"Yes, baby. I know that. Why'd you ask?"

"I just don't want you to ever forget how much I love you."

"What do you mean, don't forget?"

"I just want you to know that."

"Are you going somewhere?"

"No, Gram. I just want you to know that you are so special to me. That's all."

"Are you okay?"

"Yes. Nothing's wrong. In church, the pastor said you should always tell your loved ones how much you love them. So I'm doing that."

"Is that so?"

Granny did not like the feel of the conversation. But she tried to understand. She would mention it to her daughter, Mary.

Mary, John and Kelly had a great time visiting and then decided to go home. They'd had a great family weekend.

Everybody was happy. John was proud of his beautiful daughter. She was hanging in there like a champ. They went home and watched television until they all retired to bed. It had been a great day.

CHAPTER 9

The week went by quickly. Kelly received her tutoring and did well. She thanked her tutor for being helpful, patient and a person she felt she could talk to. She had been home schooled ever since getting out of the hospital, and she was trying to keep her grades up. She would start her new school in the second semester.

Her tutor thanked Kelly for the kind words. They finished out the rest of the week, and the tutor reminded Kelly how important it was for her to remain strong, faithful and persevering. She told her that she was a beautiful girl. Kelly thanked her for the accolades. They hugged and promised to see each other the following week.

Now it was the big day. Kelly ran upstairs and pulled out the outfit that she had planned to wear. She had asked her mother to drop her off at Starbucks and wait there until her new friend showed up. She told her mother that she had met a boy named Nicholas on the Internet. Her mother was against it, but Kelly pleaded.

"He seems like a good person. We are meeting at Starbucks, since it is so close. I told him he had to meet you."

"I want to see his driver's license and student ID."

"I don't think he drives, but I am sure he has a student ID."

"Kelly, you know the Internet can be dangerous. You have to be careful when meeting folks that way. They are never who they claim to be. I don't like this. So trust me, I am going with you."

"I understand. We talked about this at school and in our church Bible class. The Internet can be extremely dangerous, but it is a wonderful tool for information. I know you should be careful regarding the people you meet on the Internet. That is why I chose an open, public place. It is safer."

Finally, after much discussion, Kelly went into Starbucks to meet her friend. Her mother waited in the car so that she could meet the young man. After sitting in the car for more than two hours, she went into the coffee shop.

"Kelly, is he here yet?"

"Do you see him, Mom?" Kelly was clearly upset and on the verge of tears. She had been stood up, and she was hurt and depressed. She felt so unloved!

"Honey, it's okay. Let's go."

"Mom! Oh, Mom!" Kelly was nearly hysterical. Tears streamed down her face and left tracks through her makeup. "Why, Mom? Why?"

Mary tried to soothe her daughter's broken spirit, but it was hard. Over and over again, Kelly's heart was broken by people she put her faith in.

Mary was tired. Tired of seeing her daughter's tears. Tired of seeing her daughter's beautiful, bright doe eyes looking as if a shade was pulled down over them. She grabbed her daughter and pulled her to her bosom. She wanted to comfort her, but right now she wanted to get her home even more.

As Mary helped Kelly into the car, she tried to talk to her. "Let's talk about how you are feeling, sweetheart."

"There's nothing to say. I am worthless!"

"That is not true! You are a beautiful, smart and loving person. Don't let anyone make you doubt that."

"You always say that, but I continue to get hurt."

"I know I say it a lot. There is nothing wrong with the truth."

"I don't want to talk."

"Kelly, tomorrow we will go and talk to Dr. Smith."

"There is nothing she can say to me to make me feel better."

"Did you take your pill?"

"No, I stopped taking them."

"Why, Kelly? You can't stop taking your medication."

"I felt happy. Isn't that what they were for? To make me feel better?"

"You can't stop taking medicines because you want to. This is something we must tell the doctor in the morning. This is serious."

"This is not serious. Being stood up, teased, beaten, put down, kicked, stomped, spit on, talked about, pushed–that is serious. That is painful. I'm done!"

"Give yourself time. Things will change. You'll see."

"Whatever."

Mother and daughter rode in silence. Mary was troubled about her daughter. She needed help. This was not a simple matter. This was heart-wrenching. Her daughter was suffering and might even need hospitalization. Tomorrow, somehow, she would get Kelly the help she needed. She was not doing well. Bullying was destroying her self-esteem. Mary had to save her.

As they pulled into the driveway, Kelly jumped out of the car and ran quickly to her room. She slammed the door and turned on her computer. As she sat and waited, she thought about all the stuff she had experienced that had broken her young, tender heart. When the computer finally loaded up, she went to her favorites. Up popped Nicholas' MySpace page. She immediately typed an instant message.

"Nicholas, what happened?"

"What do you mean?"

"We were supposed to meet at Starbucks today at six p.m."

"Why would I schedule a time to meet you?"

"What are you talking about? We had a date to finally meet each other."

"Are you out of your freaking fat ass mind?"

"Why are you treating me like this? I thought we were friends."

"With friends like you, who needs enemies?"

"Oh, my God! I thought we were friends. Why are you hurting me like this? Why?"

"Because you are fat and ugly, and the world would be better off if you were dead."

With that, Kelly sat on the bed and cried. Her phone rang and she grabbed it. "Hello!" she screamed into the receiver."

"You fat slob," Karen and Samantha screamed.

Kelly slammed the phone down and cried until there were no more tears. Finally, she got up off her bed and grabbed her sheet. Tossing it over the bar in her closet, she stood on a chair and tied the sheet tightly around her neck. Then she kicked the chair away. She let all her dreams, tears, pain, heartache and contempt swing out of her system as she struggled, allowing the life to seep out of her body. She whispered, "Mom, Dad, I love you. Please don't hurt. Please forgive me." With her last breath, she whispered, "Please, God, forgive me!"

CHAPTER 10

Mary sat on the couch, thinking. She had just called the doctor's exchange and informed the operator that she had an emergency and needed to talk to Dr. Smith. As she waited for the doctor to call, John walked into the house.

"Honey, we need to talk. Kelly had a very bad day."

John listened to his wife tell him about what had happened to Kelly. In his anger and desire to comfort his daughter, he hopped off the couch and rushed up the stairs. Mary was right on his heels.

Grabbing the door and twisting the knob, John found the door locked. "Kelly, honey, please open the door for Dad." No sound. "Kelly, sweetheart! Please open the door for Dad." More silence. He began to bang on the door. "Open the door, Kelly!" Nothing. This frightened him. He backed up and kicked the door in. When he saw her, he started screaming. "No, Kelly! No!" He rushed and tried to lift her up to stop her from choking, but it was too late. Kelly was dead. Nothing could help her.

****

In all the pain and confusion, Mary and John made funeral arrangements for their only child. It was as if they were walking around in a haze. The pain was so great that they could not understand or conceptualize how they would survive it.

Everyone called to offer their condolences, but nothing mattered. Nothing. They'd lost their only child, and they could not imagine how they would move on. But they knew they had to, because they did not want this to happen to anyone else.

After John and Mary had found Kelly, they'd seen the instant messages still on the screen. They would find Nicholas. He needed to know that he had their daughter's blood on his hands. But right now, they were all heading to the church to celebrate Kelly's life on earth. As people lined up outside the church, Mary noticed that there were more than a thousand people waiting. Most of them were teenagers. She decided that she would speak at the service, even though she had not planned to.

Everyone walked into the church and were seated. The service began. A young woman from the choir sang a beautiful, powerful song. The song was titled "Faith." It was soothing. As the service continued, a young girl Kelly often talked to at church went up to read a poem she'd written. The girl, Mikita Williams, and Kelly had planned to go skating and to start spending time together. Mikita's poem was called "Starting Over."

No longer am I trapped, I've let myself free.
I've realized that the only person that can change me is me.
I'm not going to cry or any of that.
I'm just saying, in my life this is where I'm at.
I've been hurt in so many ways,
But I can stand here with pride and say that I'm okay.
I feel that I have the luck of a four-leaf clover,
So as of right now I am starting over.

The poem was so powerful. As Mikita spoke, no other sound could be heard. Everyone in the audience held their breath. It was so inspiring, so real, as if Kelly had breathed her words right into Mikita's mouth.

As Mikita walked to her seat, everyone clapped their approval. Next in the order of service were the words of expression. At least ten students went up to speak. They told of how sweet Kelly was, but how they never really reached out to her because they were too busy. One young lady asked the teens in the audience to help other teens, because no one else could understand the pain that teens go through.

Finally, Mary walked up. She did not plan it. She had to talk and express her feelings. She began, "Bullying is the act of using words or actions to have power over another person. When I was little, we would sing this song called 'Sticks and Stones.' It went something like this: *Sticks and stones may break my bones, but words will never hurt me.*

But words do hurt. Not only do they hurt, they kill. There are many ways that words hurt: when you call people names; when you write mean, untruthful things; when you leave people out of activities; when you don't talk to them; when you threaten them, make them feel scared, uncomfortable, or sad. Other ways you hurt people include kicking, hitting, making them do things they don't want to do, or even taking their personal belongings. This is bullying. To the ones you are bullying, it is like you are killing them. Every single day that you hurt them, you take more of their self-esteem. You kill their dreams. When you are doing this, it may be fun for you, but for the person who is on the receiving end it is harmful. It hurts the person so deeply, it's hard to bring her out of that pain."

The audience was so quiet, but Mary knew she had to keep going. There were more than five hundred teens in the audience. Where were they when Kelly needed a friend? Mary had to stop them from hurting another child.

"Has anyone ever hurt you? Have any of these negative things happened to you, or your sister, or your friend? Have you been a victim or a perpetrator? Bullying someone is wrong. It must be stopped. People bully others because they want to look cool, tough, or like they are in charge, or like they have no worries, or because they simply want to be popular. They do it for attention, or simply because they want someone to be afraid of them. People who were bullied often become bullies. You wonder why someone would want another person to hurt like they did. It's a cycle, like abuse. It is a learned behavior that needs to be changed."

"Talk to us!" a parent in the audience shouted.

"There are many reasons folks bully people, but Kelly was bullied for no particular reason. She was a loving child. She would do anything for others. She didn't deserve the pain she was put through daily. I say this not to hurt you. That is not my intention. I want it to stop, so that no other teen will ever experience the pain and alienation my child suffered.

"Finally, it is important that each of you understand this new type of bullying. It is called cyber-bullying. This means using the computer to bully folks. Using high technology to threaten, insult, or harass. Some people are using technologies like cell phones and the Internet to hurt and malign people. Using technology does not prove your strength and it does not provide physical contact, but it is as harmful as face-to-face bullying, or even more harmful. People use cyber-bullying because it is quick. They can disguise themselves or become anyone they wish to be. Using the Internet to bully, they can spread rumors quickly."

"Amen," said the pastor of the church.

"Bullying is very harmful. Some people can't take it. It makes people feel useless, devalued, unhappy and scared. The victims feel scared and unsafe, like they've done something wrong. They shouldn't have to feel that way.

"Please don't let my daughter's death be in vain. If you know that someone is being bullied, tell an adult–someone like a teacher, a pastor, or a principal. Also, it wouldn't hurt to make the person who's bullied feel good about herself or himself. If you stand by and laugh and participate, that's like saying you agree with the bullies. Plus, it keeps the bullying going. If you are a bully, most people don't like you, anyway. They know you are weak and hate yourself. People who bully others have problems. If you know a bully, ask what is wrong with him."

"Amen, sister," the pastor said as he clapped his hands.

"My daughter was loved. She had a family who loved her dearly. Please, never bully anyone."

As Mary walked to her seat, the crowd of mourners rose to their feet in a thunderous round of applause. The clapping was deafening, yet it was sad. Mary's speech, although unprepared, had helped someone in the crowd. Kelly's death would not be in vain.

****

Six months after Kelly died, her mother investigated Nicholas' identity. What she found would break any mother's heart. Karen Patrick's mother, Teresa, was identified as portraying Nicholas. Apparently, Teresa, Karen and Samantha had played a terrible joke on Kelly. As an adult, Teresa should have been ashamed of her antics. But since she did not appear remorseful, Mary and John vowed to lobby to change laws on cyber-bullying. They also decided to file a lawsuit and press charges against Teresa for fraud.

Poems

By Mikita Williams

Intelligent Death

The rain falls deeply into the skin of those who are silent but aware.

It makes the people who are loud even louder.

Even though you have a mouth, you really don't care.

You are guided into the darkness when the light is right there.

They are proud on the outside, but underneath they are dead flowers.

They may act electromagnetic, but they have no power.

They may rejoice and sing, but are tired the next hour.

They might push out so much, but go down the drain like showers.

But others, they laugh; there's no seriousness around.

They hear them moaning and love the sound.

They predict their future and control the past.

They tell them how much time they have left and hope they don't last.

They make it hard and make it so dark.

They make them feel like empty amusement parks.

They make them feel pricked and pinched

Like sorrow-filled kids that warm the bench.

So they feel suicidal and want to slaughter

And drain themselves of all that water.

The World Will Become

Let fire burn within the soul of the forgotten.

Let the remembered step aside and all turn rotten.

Smack the face of hope and shake hands with hate.

Open the door for sorrow and close the window for faith.

Let us kill happiness and save pain,

Turn your back on joy and be loyal to shame.

If we all stick together, we will be worthless.

If we stay by ourselves, we will be fine.

Unspoken Thoughts

If someone tells you they are about to die, believe them.

Even if you don't see any fainting acts.

They are hurt internally.

They are dying inside.

What people don't know is that people have feelings just as well as the next person.

I don't have internal death, well, not yet.

There will come a time where my heart will expire internally.

I will not die but I will become the dead.

My soul will evaporate right into the clouds of misery and hopelessness.

That's what people think, anyway, so I just think back.

I Lost My DNA To Life!

I shook hands with life.

I touched this hand over and over.

Life tricked me, it took my DNA.

It gave it to shame and shame gave it to sorrow.

They made my identity look like a fool.

Life let me think I was welcomed with warm hands.

Life made me think I was accepted.

Now I know I don't belong here.

I can't be friends with life.

Life is too much of a back-stabber.

First you're happy, then you're upset.

So don't let life get you like it got me.

Keep your DNA!

Photography Phonics Fundamentals
written specifically for Images of Grace,
Grace Hill Settlement House

Take a photo and you will see how beautiful life can really
be.
Keep your camera in the dark and your eyes of grace will
lose their spark.
Visualize an ancient sight and see how the dark can become
the light.
Let your creativity become true; turn something old into
brand new.
Don't just look at something and say it's boring; it can
become amazing and real adoring.
A stone into a heart, rotten into new–all the imagination
starts in you.
Realize the history within the eye; make an old well not run
that dry.
Turn a frown into a smile; make a baby demon into a loving
child.
Turn fire into a burst of colors. You can become a real
photographer lover.

BIOS

Mrs. Rose Jackson-Beavers is an advocate for teenagers as well as a motivational speaker, trainer, and the owner of Prioritybooks Publications. Prioritybooks is a publishing company that helps first time authors achieve their dreams of becoming published. She has written six books through her publishing company. Currently, she is a free-lance writer.

Some of her many accomplishments include sponsoring the first Drug-Free after Prom Dance; more than 100 high school couples attended. She coordinated the first Fresh Air Fund in the Metro-East area for pre-teens with the East St. Louis Chambers of Commerce. The Fresh Air Fund is an independent not-for-profit agency originating in New York City which provides free summer vacations to children.

Mrs. Beavers received her Bachelor's degree from Illinois State University and Masters Degree from Southern Illinois University. She spends time working in her church and volunteering at local organizations throughout her community.

She resides in Florissant, Missouri with her family.

Edward Booker

Nineteen-year-old Edward Booker loves to write and tell stories of hope, pain, and love to help educate teens and parents about life from a young perspective. Currently, he is planning to complete his education. Edward loves to make musical beats, write poetry, and hang out with his friends when he is not at the computer. He has written two additional books with plans to release *Knocked Up*, January 2010.

He resides in East St. Louis, Illinois with his family.

Introducing Poet: Mikita Williams

Mikita Williams, a 16-year-old student attending Vashon High School. She will be a junior this fall. She loves to play basketball and is a very sincere and intelligent young lady who is able to multi-task her responsibilities with easiness. She lives in St. Louis, Missouri with her family.

OTHER BOOKS FOR TEENS BY PRIORITYBOOKS

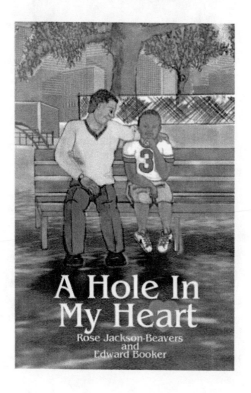

Have you felt lost and hurt thinking that your problems were so big that they couldn't be fixed? Darrius McMillan, who is 13 years old, couldn't see the love and support he had in his life because he was so blinded by what he didn't have. While going through trials with a mother who used drugs, death and sickness, he found his strength in the love of his grandmother.

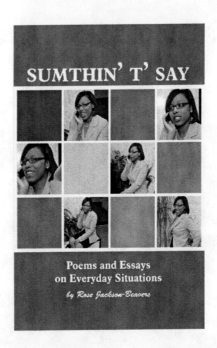

Sumthin' T' Say - is a collection of colorful, stimulating and electrifying articles and poetry about everyday life experiences. Everyone who reads "Sumthin T' Say will come away thinking about Rose's hard hitting articles and her electrifying poems which convey real emotions about Love, Life and Pain.

The first book from author Lydia M. Douglas outlines
effective strategies and goals to help students accomplish
their dreams. Relevant to students of all ages, Douglas sets
out to motivate, stimulate and inspire students, parents
and teachers to strive for the highest levels of achievement.
Stepping Stones is an effective resource for any student –
whether struggling or at the top of the class.

Reaching Higher Heights, the second book from author Lydia M. Douglas, outlines effective strategies and goals to help students accomplish their dreams. Relevant to students of all ages, Douglas sets out to motivate, stimulate and inspire students, parents and teachers to strive for the highest levels of achievement. She encourages young people to dress for success and start thinking about a saving plan for their future. It can start with small change

Coming Dec 2009

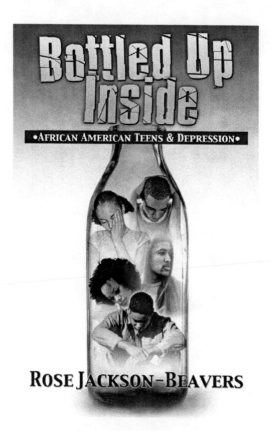

The question is asked, "Why are so many African American children giving up on life?" "Why are they failing and dropping out of school before they reach 10th grade?" When this question is posed to teenagers, the answers they give are varied. Issues like loneliness, poor home life, absent parents, lack of employment opportunities, and a sense of hopelessness seems to prevail. It is believed that many of our children are suffering from depression. This book addresses depression and how parents can address teens who may have gone undiagnosed.

LaVergne, TN USA
17 September 2009
158190LV00001B/37/P